REVIE

THIRTY DAYS DAYS

To

FOREVER

SHAYLA KERSTEN

From Thirty Days To Forever
ISBN-13: 978-1456592356
ISBN-10: 1456592351

Thirty Days
Originally published in electronic format by Liquid Silver Books, imprint of Atlantic Bridge Publishing 2006

Forever
Sequel to *Thirty Days*
Originally published in electronic format by Liquid Silver Books, imprint of Atlantic Bridge Publishing 2007

Manufactured in the United States of America
Editor: Vikky Bertling
Cover Art and Book Design: April Martinez

DEDICATION

To Myla Jackson and Delilah Devlin
for encouragement and guiding me
down the path toward publication.

To Layla Chase for her patience in teaching self-editing to the new girl and saying, "go for it."

To the Mt. Helicon Muses
for more than I can possibly fit here.

TABLE OF CONTENTS

THIRTY
DAYS

Chapter One

Biton Savakis hungered. Not for food in the normal understanding of the word. His body craved a different sustenance, a different feeding. Three months ago, his pet, his adored and much loved slave, died. Biton couldn't save him, nothing could. The cancer came on Erik quickly and, in spite of Biton's wealth and influence, the prognosis was hopeless.

To the end, Erik remained a faithful slave; never once giving in to Biton's attempts to adjust their relationship for the sake of his health. Nothing made Erik happier than serving him, and finally Biton quit trying. Whatever made Erik happy, he would give him for whatever time he had left.

Once Erik was gone, Biton's desire to rule someone went with him. Until tonight.

———

Biton entered the establishment with more than a little trepidation. His discomfort didn't show—it couldn't. As an experienced Dom, he would never allow his feelings to show, but the idea of being with someone other than Erik was more daunting than he expected. A hush fell over the few people there as they turned to look at him. A glance around the darkened room revealed a couple of familiar faces.

Nodding in his direction, the other patrons turned back to their own business.

So early in the evening there wouldn't be many here which is why Biton decided to come in now. Too many questions, too many sorrowful looks—he couldn't handle the pity.

The club hadn't changed. The dark paneling and bad lighting made it difficult to see more than the pitted dark wood of the bar. Smoke stung his eyes as he walked through the room.

Biton nodded to the bartender. "Scotch, straight up."

"Biton, my friend, how are you?"

Turning toward the familiar voice, he found Antonio Casala leading his slave, Lia, over.

A strong hand gripped his shoulder but Biton shrugged it off. "I've been better. It's been rough." Biton took a sip of the scotch to ease his tightening throat. The sympathetic gesture made it too easy to give in to what he could only do in the privacy of his own home. He appreciated Antonio's kindness and he knew the man understood his loss.

The silent long legged woman standing nearby had been with Antonio longer than the ten years Erik was with Biton. She was in remission from breast cancer. If anyone could understand, it would be Antonio.

"Maybe this was a bad idea." Biton threw back the rest of his scotch. The sound of the empty glass on the bar seemed loud.

"You need to get out. It's been months."

"I know but…" Once again, Biton's throat tightened. His eyes closed against the sting of tears. "Not here."

"Okay, how about my place. Friday night. I'm having a party. There'll be several unattached people there."

Biton nodded sharply. He knew what kind of party Antonio meant. Maybe he could shed the tension threatening to tear him apart.

"Friday." Biton should say more but he couldn't. Walking quickly to the door, he beat a hasty exit.

———

Antonio watched his friend flee from his memories. Too bad it wasn't that easy. Biton needed to move on. As a Dom, Antonio understood the need to control his life. Erik's death was the one thing Biton hadn't counted on.

"Lia."

"Yes, Master."

"Plan a play party for Friday. And make sure your little friend is there."

"Yes, Master."

A slight change in her tone made him look at her. The luscious rosy lips curved slightly at the corner.

"You wish to say something?" Antonio couldn't control the grin threatening his own mouth.

"No, Master." She bit her lips to hold back her smile.

"Witch." A sharp swat to her round ass sounded loud in the quiet bar. He tugged at her collar and headed back to his table. It had been Lia's idea to introduce Cavan to Biton.

———

The king size bed swallowed Biton without the warmth of Erik beside him. It took him nearly a month to sleep in it after his lover's death. Tonight, the couch and falling asleep to the blare of the television seemed more appealing, but he stayed where he was. He needed his life back even if the hole in his soul would never be filled.

"Erik, I miss you so much," Biton whispered into the darkness as he stared toward the ceiling. "I shouldn't have gone there tonight. It wasn't right without you." Tears rolled down the sides of his face. "Antonio was there—with Lia. She looks good. Her hair's grown back out."

Erik and Lia had been closer friends than Biton and Antonio. Erik went with her for her chemo treatments when her Master couldn't be with her. Biton's beloved mourned the loss of Lia's long dark hair. Barely a year later, Lia returned the favor.

"It's almost as long as before…" The words choked him. The memory of Erik's thick dark hair, falling out by the handful, made Biton gasp in pain.

Shaving his head was added to Erik's daily grooming, along with shaving his genitals.

Pulling a pillow against his face to stifle the sobs, he mumbled, "I still love you. I just need…need to go on. I hope you understand."

Biton rolled to his side, clutching to his chest the pillow that no longer smelled of Erik. The soft cotton pillowcase muffled his sobs until he finally fell into an exhausted sleep.

—

Friday arrived too quickly for Biton. Staring at his reflection in the mirror, he looked older than his forty-two years. His coal black hair, courtesy of his Greek heritage, was starting to go salt and pepper. Even his thick chest hair showed grays spattered through it. The dark rings under his eyes attested to his inability to sleep. His muscle tone was still good. Exercise helped keep his demons at bay. He'd lost weight. Sometimes eating was too much of an effort. Besides, the kitchen had been Erik's domain. Biton felt as if he were trespassing when he cooked for himself.

The dark eyes staring back at him from the mirror were haunted and lost. Did other people see it when they looked at him?

His work as an attorney didn't hold any real interest

anymore. As a senior partner in one of the largest law firms in New York, he could afford to delegate most of his cases to others. Retiring early crossed his mind more and more these days. Money wasn't a problem. His savings and investments would keep him comfortable for years. But what would he do? Curl up in the darkness and die, most likely. Work was the only thing anchoring him to his life.

The sad dark man in the mirror shook his head and left the bathroom.

———

Biton parked on the narrow street near Antonio's brownstone. Sitting in the car, he watched several people climb the stairs to the door. He hoped there weren't many people here tonight. His hand moved to put the key back in the ignition then hesitated. Control—he needed to regain control of his life. Going to work every day and coming home to mourn Erik was not living.

Resolved to make the most of tonight, Biton climbed out of the car and took the stairs two at a time. This was a play party, he reminded himself. Maybe, just maybe, he could find someone to interest him, even if only for one night.

———

Antonio watched as Lia peeked through the blinds. Her job as the host's slave was to greet the guests and make them comfortable. Although the brownstone could accommodate more, he planned a small gathering, less than ten people. Antonio didn't want to overwhelm Biton. His gaze darted around the room until it fell on the object of his search.

Cavan had found a corner and made himself almost disappear. The slim redhead, dressed in faded jeans and an open button down shirt, looked out of place clutching the last piece of his former life. Unless a Master offered it, wearing the wide leather collar wasn't allowed. However, Cavan wouldn't leave it in his room. It had become his security blanket.

Antonio shook his head. How had he managed to end up taking in such a wounded soul?

He glanced back to the door as Lia opened it for Biton. His beautiful slave greeted their guest with the deference due a friend of her Master. Sometimes Antonio wondered just who the slave really was in their relationship. He may have control over her body but she owned his heart. She wanted to help the poor redheaded waif who sat looking lost in the corner of Antonio's living room.

Now to get Biton to notice him.

———

Biton glanced around the room to see many familiar faces. A small sigh of relief escaped his control when he noted the number. Too many people and he was afraid he would bolt.

A lump stuck in his throat with the memory of his last visit with Erik so close behind him he could smell his scent. His slave always smelled of coffee. A smile twitched at his lips. Erik had a caffeine addiction so great that, had Biton needed to punish him, denying him coffee was true torture.

"Biton! Welcome!" Antonio walked toward him, hand out.

"Thanks," Biton replied, his hand firmly clasped in Antonio's. "Small party."

"Yeah, wasn't in the mood for anything too elaborate. You should know most of the people here."

As they released hands, Biton glanced around the room again. Only a couple of people he didn't know. Possibly the unattached ones Antonio mentioned the other night.

A dark haired, dark eyed man of about thirty moved toward him. Stopping a few feet away, he maintained a respectful silence. Evidently already trained, the man kept his gaze down, his body still.

"Hi," Biton said quietly.

"Hello, may I get you a drink?"

"Scotch, straight up."

The submissive moved away quickly to fetch his drink.

Biton glanced back at Antonio. "Who is he?"

"Mark Davenport. He's new to the New York scene. Moved here from California when his firm relocated. His old Master released him from his contract. He can't be 24/7, but he has excellent references."

Biton had to smile. The S&M scene seemed so organized sometimes. Of course, it needed to be.

Although many people thought S&M was wrong and the kinkiest form of sexual gratification, there were rules. Most people abided by them and organization helped keep those who didn't from causing too much trouble. Safe, sane and consensual was their motto. But there were those who didn't follow the rules. And those were the ones the newspapers always heard about.

Biton merely nodded as the sub appeared with his drink. The man was probably mid-thirtyish, close to Erik's age. A tight t-shirt revealed taut muscles and a well-built physique. Interesting, but Mark was too close in build and body type to Erik. Biton didn't want a substitute for his slave. Something new, something different would be better. It would take his mind away from missing Erik.

"Thank you, Mark," Biton smiled at the man and turned back to Antonio. Mark's soft steps moved away.

"Well, I think you broke his heart already." Antonio's smile was teasing. "The boy's pretty desperate for a new Master. He's been here about three months. But, fortunately, he's taking the safe route and only meeting tops the Society recommends."

The Society was an unofficial official group of BDSM clubs in the area. A hierarchy existed within it and Antonio was one of its leaders. Biton had always been active in it as well until Erik became ill. BDSM could be dangerous with the wrong people. Inexperienced tops could do serious damage to their subs. Having a group to moderate play was only wise.

Biton realized another man was standing nearby.

Glancing over his shoulder, he found a blond man, thin and smooth skinned, eyes lowered, standing a few feet away. Too young for his tastes, the sub couldn't be more than twenty.

Biton turned his gaze back to Antonio. "This was a set up, wasn't it?" He let his smile soften the accusation.

Antonio shrugged. "Caught." He reached out his hand and rested it on Biton's shoulder. "Since you were at the club I knew you were beginning to look again. I just wanted to make it easier."

"So was that my selection?"

Antonio laughed, his hand squeezing Biton's shoulder before he released it. "No, there's one more. Couldn't offer you a blond and a brunette without throwing in a redhead! Cavan's a little shy though."

Biton turned to follow his friend's line of sight. A rather forlorn looking redhead sat with his legs curled up under him in a corner of the room.

As he walked toward the young man, Biton could see the muscle tone through the open shirt. His eyes down, Cavan obviously didn't notice Biton's approach until he was looming over him.

"I'm sorry, Ma—," the young man's voice cut of sharply as he rose from the small sofa. "May I serve you?" He was taller than he appeared while seated. Maybe it was the way he made himself smaller, curled in a tight ball.

"Relax, Cavan. I just want to talk." Biton sat down and motioned Cavan to do the same.

The young man complied, but Biton could see the

reluctance in his bearing. Tense and uncomfortable, Cavan sat on the edge of the sofa, his posture stiff. His knuckles were white as he held onto the leather collar.

"Is that your collar?"

"Yes, M…"

Once again, Cavan bit back the word. It wasn't proper to call someone Master without permission. Usually the privilege wasn't granted until an understanding was reached. But maybe he would relax a little…

"If it makes you comfortable, Cavan, you may call me Master or Sir, but it is not a contract."

"Thank you, Master." Pale green eyes darted up and the tension hardened muscles in his back softened a little. "Contract, Master?"

"A contract… Between a Master and a slave. Didn't your old Master have a contract with you?"

"No, Sir."

"An agreement, then. One about your responsibilities and his."

"My responsibility was to obey my Master in all things."

The words sounded rote.

"What about his responsibility to care for you, see to your needs?"

"My only need was to serve my Master."

"Do you have a job?"

Cavan's eyes flicked between Biton and the wide leather collar, still held in a white knuckled grip. "I do now. I serve—I work in M—Mr. Casala's house. I'm a house servant."

Biton heard the difficulty Cavan had saying Antonio's name without adding the title of Master. "But you didn't before? With your old Master?"

"No, Sir. My job was to serve him." A shudder swept down his back.

Biton glanced up to see Antonio edging closer to where he and Cavan were seated. Some questions needing asking, but getting answers out of Cavan was like pulling teeth.

"Cavan, I need another drink. Scotch, straight up."

The young man sprang like a tightly wound coil released. "Yes, Master." Relief flooded the two words as if he were desperate to serve in any capacity.

As the young man fled on his errand, Biton crooked a finger at the hovering Antonio.

"What's his story?" Biton asked as Antonio took Cavan's seat.

"His last, and only, Master was Maxwell Wainwright."

"Wainwright… the name's familiar."

"You probably got the emails about the incident from the Society, but it was only a week or so after Erik's death. I'm sure you weren't paying attention. Cavan showed up at the emergency room badly beaten. His back was a bloody mess, broken arm, two fractured ribs and rectal lacerations from some kind of foreign object. He refused to press charges against his attacker. Lia called me because she recognized the name of the man paying the bills."

He nodded as he remembered Lia was an emergency room nurse.

"Well, the Society warned Wainwright, threatened to exclude him and issue warnings to potential subs. A week later, right after he was released from the hospital, Cavan returned to the emergency room with a broken jaw and bloody nose. Wainwright had tossed him in the street with nothing but a pair of jeans, his collar and his new injuries. Lia stepped in and asked permission to bring him home."

Biton's teeth clenched in anger. No one had the right to abuse a slave. The scene was not about pain for pain's sake. The redhead couldn't have been more than twenty-five or twenty-six. "How long was he with Wainwright?"

"Since he was eighteen, nine years."

So he was twenty-seven. "Was it all like that? The abuse?" Biton watched as the young man hurried toward them, drink in hand.

"I think so. Getting him to talk is difficult. I would guess Wainwright threatened him. And he's so well trained I doubt he'd ever break his confidence." Antonio rose as Cavan drew near. "I'll talk to you later." Antonio nodded to Cavan as he walked past to mingle with his other guests.

Cavan knelt to present the drink to Biton as if he were carrying something precious and rare.

Biton took the drink with one hand and patted the cushion beside him with the other. "Thank you. Sit here. You don't have to kneel."

"Yes, Master." The young man moved with grace to comply, but his fingers once again clutched his collar.

Biton sipped his drink silently. Cavan interested him, but he was so wounded, so lost. On the other hand, maybe that's why the young man caught his interest. Biton felt the same way without Erik.

Chapter Two

Morning dawned with Biton feeling more rested than he had in a long time. He left the party before anything really began. He didn't think he was ready for anything more than socializing yet and the only person to pique his interest was the very shy redhead. Putting him through a scene in public wouldn't have been a good idea.

Pale sunlight filtered through the windows. The early spring day was supposed to be clear and warmer than normal. Biton had a lunch date to look forward to. Getting information out of Cavan last night was like playing twenty questions. The pale young man would only answer direct questions. Biton wanted to learn more. Instead of continuing their stilted conversation, he asked Cavan to have lunch with him. Maybe without the crowd of people watching them, Biton could get more answers.

THIRTY DAYS

The clock showed almost nine. Biton stretched lazily and stared at the ceiling. Between his curious mind mulling over Cavan and the several scotches he'd consumed last night, he hadn't had his nightly conversation with Erik.

"He needs someone." Biton whispered. "And so do I. I know you understand. It doesn't mean I don't miss you. I'll always love you." The familiar sting of tears made him blink rapidly. "Maybe helping him to heal will help me too."

Rolling out of bed, Biton headed for the shower. He hadn't decided where to take Cavan for lunch. Bringing him here wasn't a good idea. The young man might read too much into it. Lunch in a quiet public place would be a better idea. Some place not too threatening, not related to the scene would probably be better, but Cavan's tendency to subservience could get embarrassing. Erik had shown deference to Biton at home or in the clubs or the homes of like-minded friends, where it was appropriate.

The hot water coursing over him felt good. Standing with his palms against the front of the shower, he let the water beat down on his head. Biton's thoughts roamed back to Cavan. The pale face, with its spattering of freckles and its sad green eyes, had flitted through his dreams. Cavan's almost natural deference and submissiveness made his cock take interest as well.

The idea of him spread-eagled for Biton's pleasure caused a gasp of excitement. His dick swelled as Biton imagined freckles across the younger man's back and ass. With his coloring, the man was obviously a natural redhead, but Biton wondered if Cavan's groin was shaved or if the hair there would be the same color as his head. The open shirt Cavan wore last night revealed a hairless chest, smooth muscles and tiny pink nipples. No visible piercings, not even his ears. Cavan's lips were a little less full than he liked—than Erik's were—but they still tempted him.

Biton hadn't had a satisfactory orgasm since before Erik died. Masturbating for the sake of getting off just didn't interest him. On the rare occasion when he had gotten hard, it usually fizzled before he ever came. But the idea of those pale green eyes looking up at him, with Cavan's lips wrapped around his cock, made him reach for his now swollen erection. A few hard strokes and Biton watched his seed circle the drain of the shower and wash away.

Maybe his place would be a better place for lunch. If it turned into something more than lunch…

The door to Antonio's brownstone opened before Biton had the chance to knock. As Biton entered, Cavan stood quietly to the side.

Antonio waited in the living room with Lia. "Welcome, my friend." He grasped Biton's hand firmly.

Lia smiled and bowed her head in greeting.

Antonio turned to Cavan. "Go get your jacket. It's still cool outside."

They all watched as the young man hurried from

24

the room.

"Go ahead, Lia." Antonio's voice was quiet as he gave her permission to speak.

"He's extremely nervous, but very excited. I've been trying to counsel him, but he's so lost without a Master." Lia kept her voice low as she addressed Biton. "I don't know where you plan to take him, but I wouldn't recommend any place in public outside the scene."

"I already thought of that. I decided we'd have lunch at my house." Biton looked anxiously at the hallway where Cavan disappeared.

Lia nodded her approval. "It will probably be better. He's almost agoraphobic. I don't think his Master allowed him out of the house."

"Okay, I'll be careful, Lia. Thanks."

Their conversation was cut short with Cavan's return.

———

Biton mused over Lia's words on the drive back to his house. What was he getting himself into?

A glance over at Cavan revealed a frightened young man, his hand inside his jacket pocket surely gripped around his collar.

Deciding against talking in the car, Biton drove in silence for the rest of the trip.

Relief showed as Cavan's posture relaxed a little when they pulled into the garage. The big sigh almost made Biton grin.

The decision to eat here was definitely the best idea. Biton had ordered a cold meal from a local restaurant. The table was already set and the food was in the refrigerator.

"Have a seat. I'll get the food." Biton moved to the refrigerator, but Cavan's tension escalated.

The knots in his neck and gritted teeth showed Cavan's discomfort with someone waiting on him.

"On second thought, take this." He handed the distressed young man the platter of cold curried chicken before Biton grabbed the salad and a bottle of white wine.

After allowing Cavan to hold his chair for him, Biton motioned for the young man to take the other seat.

"Cavan, you need to listen carefully. Until we reach an agreement or a contract like I mentioned last night, you don't have to serve me. This lunch is just for us to get to know each other, to see if we want to take things further."

Cavan nodded, his muscles strained with anxiety as he perched on the chair.

"Say you understand. I want to hear you. I want you to tell me what you think, what you want. It's part of getting to know each other."

"Yes, Master, I understand."

Biton sighed and dropped the subject while he filled Cavan's plate and then his own. Even that simple gesture made Cavan jittery. What kind of monster trained him?

"Eat, Cavan. It's okay."

The pale green eyes darted from Biton to the plate of food and back again, almost as if Cavan expected it to be a trap or a joke.

Maybe this wasn't such a good idea. Biton's own psyche was too fragile dealing with Erik's loss. Having someone so frightened around... Then again, Cavan had already taken his mind off his grief for a little while.

Standing slowly so as not to startle his skittish guest, Biton circled around behind Cavan.

The muscles in his neck bulged with tension.

Gently placing his hands on Cavan's shoulders made the young man flinch, but he controlled it quickly. Rubbing the knotted shoulders with the palm of his hands, he leaned over to whisper, "Cavan, you have to relax. I'm not going to punish you for anything. You aren't mine to punish." Biton's fingers began kneading the tight flesh. "I want you to eat. I want you to talk to me. I need to know things about you, about your last Master just as you need to know things about me. You won't be in trouble for doing any of these things."

The trembling under Biton's hands started slow, but soon the young man was shaking hard.

Slipping his arms around Cavan's chest, Biton whispered, "It's okay, Cavan. It's okay."

Pulling free and practically falling out of the chair, Cavan crawled to Biton and wrapped his arms around his legs.

"I just want to serve, Master. Please... I need..."

Prying himself loose from the frantic man's iron

grip, Biton lowered himself to the floor. Wrapping his arms around Cavan, Biton pulled him up. Keeping him in a tight grip, he moved him toward the living room and the couch.

Pulling Cavan down with him, Biton held on, in spite of his weak resistance. Had Wainwright never showed him tenderness or concern?

"Cavan, calm down. I may yet let you serve me, but I want to know about you first. There are things we need to discuss." Biton didn't know if the stern tone he used did the trick or the promise he might be allowed to serve, but the feeble struggle ceased.

Cavan's body went almost limp against him, his head resting on Biton's chest.

The heat of a body against Biton awakened more than just concern for his terrified guest, but he needed to quash the feeling of arousal. Nothing helped as Biton's cock swelled against his jeans. And it didn't escape Cavan's notice.

"Please let me…" With a shaking hand, Cavan caressed the now visible bulge. "Please, Master."

The pitiful whisper tore at Biton's heart but sent heat shooting through his groin. Nodding his permission, he leaned back on the couch to see what Cavan would do.

Without attempting any other contact, a kiss or touch, Cavan slid to the floor, kneeling between Biton's legs, he opened his jeans. Freeing Biton's aching cock from his boxers, Cavan suckled the tip then licked his way around the crown. One hand slid deeper, caressing his balls as Cavan's mouth opened to take him all.

Throat muscles contracted around the sensitive head of his cock.

"Oh, God," Biton moaned. Leaning back with his eyes closed, Biton let his fingers wander through Cavan's thick short hair. It had been so long, seemed like an eternity, since he felt so good. "Yes... Oh, yes," he moaned.

Cavan's mouth slid back up to the tip. A hot tongue swiped against the sensitive slit. As timid as the man was, Cavan's mouth was just the opposite. Taking him deep again, almost aggressively, Cavan's tongue worked constantly against his cock. Biton couldn't take much more without exploding. He didn't want it to end so soon.

Tugging roughly at the soft hair in his fingers, he pulled Cavan away. Sliding his hands under Cavan's arms, he pulled him up against him. Lips clashed hard, teeth knocking together as Biton kissed him.

Cavan's mouth opened obediently but there was no passion in his lips. His arms stayed at his side, neither welcoming Biton's embrace nor defending against it.

"Kiss me, Cavan." Biton whispered. "Kiss me back."

Slowly, the soft thin lips began to move.

Biton's tongue chased Cavan's elusive one, kissing him deep and tangling with the hot moist flesh.

"Hold me," Biton whispered as he gasped for air. "Put your arms around me."

Cavan's arms obeyed but his hold was loose.

"Tighter, Cavan. Hold me tighter."

Biton reached between them and slipped open the button on Cavan's jeans. Sliding the zipper free, his hand sought the younger man's erection only to find flaccid flesh. Cupping the loose balls, his hand encountered a cock ring, so tight as to be dangerous. The blood flow to his penis and balls would be too constricted.

If he had permanent damage, Cavan was effectively a eunuch.

Biton's fingers fumbled for the release but couldn't find one. "Cavan, I want this off. How does it come off?"

The body against Biton tensed. "My Master said I couldn't take it off. Only to shave."

Biton pulled his hand free of Cavan's jeans. Using both hands to cup the pale freckled face, Biton forced Cavan to look him in the eyes.

A hasty decision but one made, nonetheless. "Cavan, listen to me carefully. He is not your Master anymore. This afternoon I'll draw up a contract between you and me outlining your responsibilities and mine." Seeing his eyes flare with hope and joy, it nearly killed Biton to put a damper on it. "It will be a temporary one. Thirty days. During this time, you are mine. You will obey me, you will follow my rules not your old Master's and you will behave as I see fit. If you don't, you will be punished. I, on the other hand, am responsible for your safety, your health and your living conditions." Squeezing Cavan's face gently, Biton continued, "Do

30

you understand what I'm saying?"

"Yes, Master." Tears filled Cavan's eyes.

"Okay, the first thing I'm ordering you to do is remove the cock ring. You will only wear one if and when I say so. Do you understand?"

"Yes, Master," Cavan said, breathless as he pulled away from Biton. Dropping his pants without hesitation or the slightest embarrassment, Cavan fumbled with the tight strap around his penis and balls. It turned out to be stretchable, like a large rubber band.

Biton shuddered at the thought. He had read once where rams were castrated using a similar method. "Take off your shoes and finish removing your jeans. I want to examine you."

Cavan quickly complied and stood in front of Biton in only his shirt and socks.

It would look silly if the situation wasn't so serious.

Biton caressed the flaccid circumcised penis, pale like the rest of Cavan's skin. Pulling the limp flesh gently first to one side and then the other, he examined the darker skin where the ring had been. Curiously, Cavan didn't react. Looking up, Biton saw the tension in Cavan's shoulders and neck. "Does my touching you hurt?"

"No, Master."

"Does it excite you at all?"

"I'm not supposed to be excited. My Master said…"

Biton slid one hand around to Cavan's ass and swatted one cheek. Excitement flowed through Biton and straight to his still hard cock. "I'm your Master now. Remember. You do as I say." Another swat for good measure sent fire through Biton.

"Yes, Master. What should I do? How can I serve?"

Holding the still limp flesh of his new slave's penis, Biton suckled gently on the tip. He could feel the shudder race through Cavan. Smiling as he pulled away, "I want you hard, aching and begging for my touch."

Slowly, the soft flesh began to stiffen.

Biton licked the head, teasing the slit with the tip of his tongue. Another hard swat brought a moan from above and further evidence Cavan's cock didn't have permanent damage.

Biton licked and nipped around the swelling crown. His fingers found the silky shaven texture of Cavan's balls irresistible. Rolling the slowly tightening sacs, Biton swallowed the rising cock, enjoying the feel of the erection hardening in his mouth.

"Master…" The word came out as a whimper, the first audible sign of Cavan's enjoyment.

Biton pulled away long enough to speak. "What, Cavan? What do you want?"

"To serve you," he moaned.

After one last taste of the hard flesh, Biton stood up. Pulling Cavan close, he kissed him hard, teeth clashing and tongue driving deep into his mouth.

The sudden move unbalanced the younger man. Instinctively he wrapped his arms around Biton to keep from falling. Their bodies met with brute force, hard cocks pressed tight between them.

Not wanting to relinquish Cavan's mouth, Biton moved them slowly toward the playroom. As he pushed the door open and manhandled Cavan through it, Biton's passion faltered briefly. Since Erik died, Biton rarely came in here. The memories were too painful.

The desperate hands clutching the back of his shirt quickly brought his mind back to the present.

Aching for relief, Biton moved Cavan to the nearest piece of equipment, a large leather sling. Pushing Cavan into it, still dressed in only his shirt and socks, Biton quickly secured his wrists and ankles in the shackles.

Bending over his now captive slave, Biton kissed him hard as his fingers tore at the buttons of Cavan's shirt. Fumbling in his desire, he straightened up, grabbed both sides of the shirt and yanked. Buttons flew exposing the pale freckled chest.

Rapid breath and clenched fists were the only signs, beyond the rigid cock, of Cavan's arousal. No moans, no pleas, no sounds. Wainwright must have required silence. Biton did not.

"Talk to me, Cavan. Tell me what you're feeling." Biton pinched a tiny nipple, a gentle nip. "Does this feel good?"

"Yes, Master."

A small moan escaped with the words and made Biton smile.

"Listen to me carefully, Cavan. I am your new Master. With the exception of obedience, all the rules Wainwright had are gone. You will learn my ways. Understand?" Biton tweaked the hardening nipple again, this time with a little more pressure.

"Yes, Master."

"One of my rules, unless I tell you to be silent, I want to hear you when we play. I want to hear your moans, your cries. How can I know what I'm doing is good for you if you don't tell me?"

"Yes, Master." This time the moan exhaled was louder.

Taking Cavan's swollen, leaking cock in his hand and stroking slowly, Biton leaned over until his lips almost touched Cavan's ear. "I want you to feel pleasure in the pain," he whispered.

"Yes... Master..."

Reaching with his other hand, Biton pinched a now tight nipple hard. "Tell me what you feel."

"G—good—Master. Good..."

The stammered word made Biton smile. He already decided to stick with pinches and openhanded blows. Until Cavan was retrained, anything rougher could be dangerous. Cavan might not tell him to stop if things went too far.

With a final twisting stroke to the leaking cock, Biton walked over to the toy chest. Small implements of pain, clamps, floggers and the like, were stored in the drawers of a tall dresser. Condoms and various lubes were stashed there as well. Grabbing lube and a condom, Biton eyed some of the nipple clamps. A pair of loose ones maybe? The kind he used as warm up for tighter ones. Snagging the clamps, he turned back to Cavan.

Tear-filled pale green eyes watched him.

"What's wrong, Cavan?" Biton strode quickly back to the sling bound slave. Depositing his goodies on the leather beside Cavan, Biton stroked the bright red hair. "Talk to me."

"My—my cock, Master. Hurts."

Kissing the tears mixed with sweat sliding down Cavan's face, Biton whispered, "When was the last time you were allowed to come?"

"Not allowed…"

"You are now." A flare of anger engulfed Biton. Sometimes Biton had denied Erik, but only to draw out the pleasure. Not allowing him to come at all was unthinkable. How could Wainwright deny his slave something so basic? The scene wasn't about torture for the sake of torture. It was about pain for pleasure in like-minded people, the pleasure of inflicting it *and* the pleasure of receiving. Biton wondered if Cavan really enjoyed pain or if he was just conditioned to it.

Grabbing the lube, Biton moved around the sling and between Cavan's legs. After lubing the fingers of his left hand, Biton reached for the swollen cock with his right. "You'll come for me." Bending his face to the angry red flesh, Biton suckled the tip as his lubed finger sought Cavan's puckered hole. "Come for me now, Cavan. I want to taste you."

Working his finger in the tight passage as his mouth sucked the head of the hot cock, Biton tasted a gush of pre-cum. His thumb pressed against the perineum as his finger searched for Cavan's prostate. Biton's other

35

hand held the base of his cock, his fingers massaging the tight balls. His mouth releasing the hot flesh, Biton whispered. "Now, Cavan. Let me taste you."

Biton's mouth barely covered the rigid shaft before the first spurt of bitter fluid shot across his tongue. Moving his mouth off again, he whispered, "Let me hear how it feels." A shot of come splattered his lips. "Let me hear you. Tell me how it feels." His mouth engulfed the hard flesh again. Biton slid a second finger in the velvet-lined passage and pressed against the hard knot of Cavan's prostate.

"Oh God—it feels so good—Master—good…"

Cavan's babbling made Biton smile around the still hard flesh. Sucking him dry, Biton added a third finger to the loosening hole. His own cock in serious need of attention, Biton released Cavan and slid his fingers from the tempting ass. Rolling on a condom and lubing himself generously, he watched the tears streaming down Cavan's face. "Are you hurting?"

Cavan shook his head no, but his tears didn't slow.

Biton leaned forward and kissed the salty liquid from his cheeks. "Do you want me to stop?"

"No, Master…"

Holding his cock steady, Biton lined up with Cavan's hole. Pushing slowly past the tight ring of muscle, Biton moaned his pleasure. "Feels good…"

Cavan took a deep breath and pushed against Biton's invading flesh.

Sliding in balls deep, Biton fought the urge to empty his seed into the velvet steel sheath. He didn't want it to end so soon. Leaning forward, his lips captured Cavan's.

Cavan's neck strained, reaching for closer contact. Pulling at his shackles, the lean muscles in Cavan's arms bulged.

The younger man's moans sent fire burning through Biton. "Talk to me, Cavan," Biton whispered, his lips grazing Cavan's. "Tell me what you feel."

"Good—so good—Master…"

Biton couldn't move faster without losing it. Tight muscles clenched around him as Cavan struggled to move against him. The younger man's still hard cock rubbed against Biton's stomach. Sliding his hands under Cavan's sweating body, Biton met his mouth with hard kisses. The coppery taste of blood from his bruised lip didn't stop Biton's assault on Cavan's mouth.

Slow steady strokes into the tight body quickly became frantic as Biton began to lose control. He ached for this; he needed this, a willing slave begging him for more, a warm body to do with as he pleased. Someone to take care of, someone to love. "Come with me, Cavan…" he whispered harshly. Biton's tears mingled with Cavan's as his body exploded. Hot sperm smeared his stomach as Cavan came again. As lost as Cavan in his own way, tears, sweat, spit and sperm mingled as Biton found life again in Cavan's body.

Chapter Three

Biton kissed Cavan's wrists as he freed them. Licking the reddened skin, he tasted the salt of sweat mixed with the musky hint of leather. Cavan watched his every move as if waiting for the other shoe to fall. Moving once more between the milky white thighs, Biton released his ankles from their restraints.

"Come here," Biton said, his arms held out to Cavan.

With a slight whimper, Cavan pulled himself up into Biton's arms.

"Hold me. I want you to."

With Biton's whispered words, Cavan's arms tightened to the point of pain. Soft whimpers turned to gentle sobs.

"It's okay. I'm going to take care of you now."

Sobs racked Cavan's body, convulsing almost to the point of hysteria.

Rubbing Cavan's back under the ragged shirt, Biton whispered, "Let it out. Things will be different, but they'll be better."

———

A hot shower later, a calmer Cavan sat on the couch curled into Biton's side with his head on Biton's chest. Dressed in his jeans and a borrowed t-shirt, Cavan seemed more comfortable than earlier, less tense at the close contact.

His arm tight around the skittish young man, Biton began to dredge for more information. "Where are you from?" Maybe simple questions would draw out more information.

"Here. New York."

Simple answers too. This could take a while. "Do you have family here?"

"No. They're all dead."

"I'm sorry. I know what it's like to lose people you love." Biton stroked Cavan's hair.

"I don't remember them."

"Who raised you?"

"Foster families."

"One or several?" No wonder he wasn't accustomed to affection. Between Wainwright and the foster care system, no wonder the man was afraid of everything.

"Six. There were six."

"How old were you when you first went there?"

"Five, I think."

Too old to be readily adoptable. Biton closed his

eyes thinking about the poor child, lost in the system. "Were your foster parents' kind?"

"I was disobedient. I had to be punished. That's why my last foster father sold me to my Master. He said he would make me obedient."

Biton struggled to keep the anger he felt from showing. "How old were you when this happened?"

"Eighteen, I think."

"You didn't know how old you were?"

"I thought I was sixteen, but my foster father said I was eighteen otherwise he couldn't have sold me." Cavan's tone was so calm, so matter of fact, as if this was the way things were supposed to work.

"How did you serve your foster father? Tell me all the things you did."

"I cleaned his house, washed his car, helped him bathe, and if I was really good, he would let me suck him. But that didn't happen too often because I was bad."

Biton closed his eyes against the sting of tears. He'd expected abuse from Wainwright, severe abuse from what Antonio said, but he didn't realize how young it had started. "Where was your foster mother? What did she do while you took… care of things?" His voice faltered as bile rose in his throat. Biton needed to know more about the man who abused Cavan. He needed to contact the police. There could be other children at risk.

"She was there. Sometimes she watched." Cavan's voice was almost confused, as if he didn't know what

40

else she would be doing.

Biton had to get up. His stomach roiled with disgust. "Excuse me, Cavan. I need to use the restroom."

The bathroom door safely closed and locked, Biton threw up what little was left in his stomach from breakfast.

———

Unable to consider food after listening to Cavan's story, Biton still insisted the young man eat.

"My stomach's a little upset. I think I'm coming down with something. Just because I can't eat right now doesn't mean you can't."

Cavan ate tiny bites. His fingers picked at the chicken while his eyes darted back and forth from his plate to Biton.

Keeping a tight rein on his stomach and his thoughts, Biton smiled at each bite, reassuring Cavan. He needed to call someone. Antonio was a cop and although he worked homicide, he would know what to do. He should get more information before he called anyone. Cavan was so uncomfortable around people it might be easier to get him to talk to Biton alone.

He wasn't even sure Cavan was his real name. Surely, someone would have been looking for him. Changing his name would have been a sensible precaution for his abusers.

"Have you always been called Cavan?"

The man nearly dropped the piece of chicken. Wild eyed with fear, a blush, a gasp of air, shook him.

"What's wrong?"

"I'm not supposed to tell."

"Your real name?"

"Cavan is my real name! My only name. My Master said so!"

Although surprised at the vehemence in Cavan's voice, Biton merely smiled. "But I'm your Master now. I need to know everything about you. Especially your real name. I need it for the contract. So I can make you mine." Not quite the truth, but Cavan wouldn't know any better.

The freckled skin alternated between flushed and pale. His breathing came in short pants as shaking hands dropped his food.

"I require it, Cavan. Any new Master would need it." Biton's tone was stern almost to the point of harsh.

"My… my… Michael." Almost hyperventilating, Cavan spit the word out.

"Your last name, too." Biton reached over to squeeze his shoulder.

"Delaney…" He gasped the word before he toppled from the chair in a dead faint.

Biton managed to move fast enough to keep him from hitting the floor too hard.

"Oh, fuck…"

———

"Where is he?" Lia's submissiveness didn't apply in nurse mode.

"Erik's room. He's still unconscious." Biton didn't

need to lead the way. Lia had been there many times when Erik was sick.

Antonio grabbed his shoulder to keep him from following. "Let her check him out. Tell me what happened."

They moved over to the couch and Biton sank into it with relief. He hadn't known what to do. Calling Antonio had been the first thing to pop into his head. "He's been so badly abused. I don't know where to begin."

"Did he tell you about what happened with Wainwright?"

His elbows on his knees, Biton buried his face in his hands. "No, before Wainwright. He lived with a foster family. The father abused him while the mother watched!"

"Oh, no... Poor kid!" Antonio paused for a moment. "Did you get a name?"

"Not the foster family, but I got his real name. It's Michael Delaney." Biton straightened up to look at his friend. "Evidently, they threatened him if he ever told it. Something so dire, he hyperventilated and passed out!"

Antonio shook his head. "After what Wainwright did to him, what could be worse?"

"I don't know. After all he's been through, I can't imagine." Biton rolled his head back stretching his aching neck. Today turned out so different from what he expected.

"I'll check with the department and see if they

can find anyone in the system by that name." Antonio took out a small notebook and a pen and scribbled something.

"Do you think they would still have a record of him?"

"Maybe. He would have been out of the system for, what, nine, ten years?"

Biton shook his head. "Possibly not that long. He said his foster father sold him to Wainwright when he was eighteen, but he thought he was sixteen at the time. The man insisted he was older."

Lia entered the room quietly and cleared her throat. Her normal submissiveness meant the crisis was over.

"How is he?" Antonio asked as both men stood up.

"Fine, his blood pressure is a little high, but it should settle down. Sleep is good for him at the moment."

Lia's words reassured him.

"Do you want us to take him back to our house?" Antonio offered.

Biton lowered his head as he thought about it. If Cavan woke up thinking Biton had banished him… "No. As long as you think he's okay. I agreed to a thirty-day contract. Though he doesn't understand the concept, it was the only way to get him to talk. He might see being sent back to you as punishment."

Lia smiled her agreement.

"You want us to stay for a while?" Antonio asked.

Biton just shook his head. With the adrenaline high from earlier crashing, he just wanted to rest.

"I'll let you know what I find out about him."

44

Antonio held his hand a few seconds longer than a normal handshake, squeezing his support before he released it.

"Thanks."

———

"Oh, God!" Biton's own voice woke him. His cock pulsed as he came, shooting into a hot eager mouth. Convulsing with aftershocks, his brain registered the fact that it wasn't a dream. "Cavan!"

"Did I please you, Master?" The pale green eyes met his for a brief second before Cavan slid off the bed to kneel next to it.

The young man was naked except for the wide leather collar Biton had first seen at Antonio's.

"Cavan, you shouldn't have done that. You have to wait until I give you permission." The stern tone couldn't be helped. If training, or retraining in Cavan's case, was to happen, discipline must start somewhere.

Cavan flinched at his tone and still on his knees, leaned forward to place his forehead on the wood floor. "I just wanted to serve you."

The sight of the pale flesh against the dark wood, so submissive, so willing, made Biton's spent flesh twitch. Slipping his hand in his boxers, he pulled his cock back through the opening. Biton couldn't believe Cavan didn't wake him when he crawled on the bed.

Sitting up and brushing the sleep from his eyes, Biton looked again. The long thick scars crisscrossing Cavan's back sent a rush of pity through Biton.

"Stand up."

Cavan stood with languid grace. His body straight and rigid except for the bowed head.

More scars, thick shiny strips of flesh ran across Cavan's ribs. The sign of a whip out of control, wrapping the body. Flaccid, dry and limp, Cavan's circumcised cock showed no sign of interest in what he had done to Biton. The groin area was completely shaven, as well as his balls. Several scars on his pelvis region looked circular, cigarette burns or maybe cigars. They looked too large for cigarettes. In his lust driven haste earlier, Biton hadn't noticed them.

"Turn around."

More scars, more pain. Once again, Biton wondered if Cavan enjoyed pain or was he just used to it?

Biton's gaze wandered back up the marks on Cavan's back and rested on the wide leather collar. Too tight and made of rough leather, it had to be painful and probably dangerous. Everyday collars were proof of ownership not methods of torture. Some Tops used tighter ones as a means to a pleasurable end, but those were play collars. Biton didn't have any of those. Erik never liked erotic asphyxiation. The collar Erik loved, and was buried in, was a loose, solid, thin metal circle. Biton's pet loved the sound of the chain clinking on his collar, the slink of the metal sliding across metal. Biton closed his eyes against the grief the memory stirred.

Opening his eyes, he stared at Cavan's collar. Biton had some of Erik's packed in storage but not here. Still, he didn't want Cavan wearing his former Master's.

"Take off your collar."

Cavan turned to face him, reluctance furrowed his brow for a brief second. Hesitation, slight but there, slowed Cavan's hands. Opening the buckle, his fingers fumbled. A slow red blush started up Cavan's chest as the clasp finally yielded.

"Come here. On the bed."

This time Cavan didn't hesitate. Kneeling on the mattress with his head bowed, his tongue darted out to wet his lips, his fingers still tight around his collar.

Biton held his hand out for the thick piece of leather and Cavan laid it on his palm. "You don't get a collar until you earn it. And it certainly won't be this one. A collar is the Master's choice, not yours." Biton tossed the offending piece of leather on the nightstand. "And you are mine now. Remember that. Your old Master's rules do not apply here. If you aren't sure of something, you have to ask me. Do you understand?"

Cavan nodded slightly.

"Say it, Cavan."

"I understand, Master."

Biton reached out, his hand stroking a freckled arm. The chilled flesh startled Biton. He didn't think Cavan could have gotten cold so quickly. "How long were you here? Before I woke?"

"I don't know, Master."

"What were you doing?"

"Watching you, Master. Waiting to please you."

Biton closed his eyes and drew a deep breath before he asked the next question. "Why?" He already knew the answer.

"Because it's what I'm supposed to do."

When he opened his eyes, Biton merely nodded. "Get under here." He lifted the covers to let Cavan slide next to him.

The cold body was stiff, uncomfortable.

"Come here," Biton whispered. "And relax."

Cavan slid closer, but "relax" wasn't in the young man's vocabulary.

Wrapping his arms around the lean body, Biton sighed. It would be a difficult road retraining Cavan. Nevertheless, a path that gave Biton something to look forward to for the first time since Erik died.

———

Cavan tried to keep his eyes open as the heat from his Master's body warmed him. Panic floated at the edges of his mind. The Master wanted him here, in his bed, but Cavan couldn't understand why. So many things had changed.

Lia said the change was good, that his old Master was an evil man. Cavan had never seen Mr. Casala hurt Lia, not like…

Pain flooded his memory, the burning strike of the lash as it ripped his skin open, the searing smell of burning flesh. A shiver of fear lay coiled in his gut, but he wouldn't let it out. His new Master lay silent beside him. Cavan shouldn't disturb him.

All the questions earlier terrified him, but Master Biton making him leave would be more frightening. In the few memories of his childhood he could conjure, Cavan was always alone. Most of his foster parents didn't pay him any attention. It wasn't until the last one that anybody seemed to notice him. At first, Cavan resisted what his foster father wanted, but it was less painful than the beatings. And then Master Wainwright… He had paid plenty of attention that night…

Master Biton shifted in his sleep, pulling Cavan tighter. "Erik…" The whisper was almost inaudible.

Cavan didn't resist his Master's grip. His head rested cautiously on the hair-covered chest. Warm and lost in the sound of a gentle heartbeat, Cavan couldn't keep his eyes open any longer. In his dreams, Master Biton whispered his name with the same tenderness.

———

Biton's eyes flew open. In his dream, Erik's dark eyes had turned pale green. The warm body next to him was too slight to be his love's. Memory returned and Biton stifled a sob. Not wanting to disturb the sleeping redhead, Biton eased out from under his slender body. Seated on the edge of the bed, he studied the sleeping man.

Almost delicate features, a slightly upturned nose, covered in freckles and a wide mouth. Cavan's looks weren't striking or exceptional, but he had an air of innocence about him that contradicted the hell he'd lived until now.

Biton pinched the bridge of his nose attempting to push away a forming headache. He wasn't sure he was up to the task of retraining Cavan. For all he knew, the younger man would never be able to enjoy the lifestyle he'd been forced to live. But would he be able to live any other way after so many years of abuse?

The sun was almost set. They had slept the afternoon away. Slipping silently out of the room, Biton wondered if Antonio had a chance to find out anything about Cavan's past. He wasn't sure he wanted to know more.

With an angry rumble, his stomach reminded him of his neglect and his missed meal. Dressed in only his boxers, Biton rummaged through the cabinets to see what he could fix for a meal. Besides a course for dinner, he needed a course of action for Cavan.

The phone startled him out of his thoughts. He lunged for it, not wanting Cavan disturbed by the noise.

"Hello!" Biton winced at his sharp tone.

"Am I disturbing you?" Antonio's voice chuckled with amusement.

"No, sorry. Cavan's asleep. I didn't want the phone to wake him."

"Still? Does Lia need to check him out again?"

"He was awake for a little while." Biton didn't really want to go into details about what he was doing. "Have you seen his scars?"

"Lia told me about them. Bad."

"Yeah…" Biton sighed softly. "The more I think about it, the more I wonder if I can handle it. He's so… I promised Cavan thirty days and I'll give it to him but…"

"I know. I came down to the station after I left your place."

"Did you find anything?"

"In October of 1992, Michael Delany was listed with Children's Services as a runaway at the age of eleven. He disappeared off the radar screen."

"Eleven?" A quick mental calculation put Cavan at twenty-five. If he was with Wainwright for nine years, he was sixteen when sold, just as Cavan thought. "He remembers six sets of foster parents. One of them, he was with when he was sixteen. They couldn't have been in the system if he was listed as missing in '92."

"I've called Special Victims. This is their thing, but I'll come with them to interview him."

"When? I don't know if he's stable enough to handle the pressure. He passed out when I made him tell me his name." Biton wasn't sure if this was a good idea. Maybe they should wait.

"The longer we wait more children could be at risk."

"Reading my mind, Antonio?"

"Look, I know it's going to be difficult, but it has to be done. I don't think the foster parents will be as tough as Wainwright. We need to talk to him about that as well since it appears Wainwright took him while he was underage. And the man should know who he paid for Cavan. Of course, the hard part is convincing a jury it wasn't consensual."

"Yeah, that will be difficult. He has no idea anyone

has done anything wrong. He's conditioned to believe he's a slave for his Master's pleasure and nothing more. To him, there's nothing unusual happening." Biton rubbed the heel of his palm against his forehead. The headache was starting to throb. "When?"

"Tomorrow morning. We'll come by there rather than traumatizing him by bringing him to the precinct. Nine o'clock?"

"I'm not sure I can handle this, Antonio. Maybe I've gotten in over my head with Cavan." Between the disturbing events of the day and his headache, Biton couldn't think straight.

"Sure you can. You're one of the top lawyers in the city. You can handle anything. Besides, if we don't take care of this…"

"I know. I know. I need to go. Thanks for everything." Biton pushed the off button on the phone before Antonio had a chance to say anything else.

A selfish little voice in his head warned Biton this could bring his private life further into the open than he wanted. His partners in the law firm knew he was gay, but only one knew the other part of his lifestyle. If this got into the press, it could cause irreparable damage to the firm's reputation.

Biton shook his head and leaned against the counter. With his eyes closed, the sad freckled face hovered in his vision. He had to look at the big picture. Others like Cavan were probably out there somewhere.

The firm would survive. He could retire. It's not as if he hadn't already thought about it. At least finding the abusive foster parents and seeing Wainwright behind bars was a better reason than giving up on life. Decision made him open his eyes to see Cavan standing naked in the bedroom doorway. Biton tried to smile at the bewildered young man. "Did you sleep well?"

Cavan swallowed hard and nodded. "Yes, Master."

His refusal to call Biton anything but master was going to make tomorrow difficult. "We need to talk, but first we need to find you some clothes."

Chapter Four

Cavan looked anything but comfortable in an old pair of Erik's sweats. Perched on the edge of the couch, his back straight but his head bowed, Cavan appeared ready to flee.

Biton sat down on the coffee table facing him. "Cavan, there will be some people here tomorrow to see you."

A fleeting shudder started in the slim body but stopped quickly. "I will please them as you wish, Master."

Biton shook his head. He should have known Wainwright would have shared his slave. "They just want to talk and I require you to answer them honestly."

"What about?" Cavan's breathing increased, almost panting.

"About your foster father and about your old Master." Biton kept his voice stern. This would be the first true test of Cavan's obedience. "Do you understand?"

Cavan's fingers twisted the material of the sweat pants. "Yes, Master." The acknowledgment a mere whisper as his shoulders shook. "Yes, Master."

"Cavan, my name is Biton. Say it."

"Master Biton."

"No, just my name." Biton stood up and then moved to the couch next to Cavan. "Listen to me." He twisted his body so he could study Cavan's profile. "These people tomorrow, I would prefer they not know I'm your Master. Because of my business, my work, I need you to do this. If you can't say my name, then don't call me anything. It would be easier if you could call me Biton." He ran a hand down Cavan's tense back. "Try it."

"Biton..." The whispered word sounded like a caress.

"Good." He reached for Cavan's chin, his fingers tugged until Cavan faced him. Leaning in, Biton placed a soft kiss on Cavan's lips. "Very good."

———

Biton settled back on his bed with an exhausted sigh. Strange he was so tired since he slept most of the afternoon. The stress of the situation wasn't helping. He saw Cavan tucked into Erik's bed and instructed him to stay there. He made it very clear he didn't want a repeat of this afternoon. The man's mouth was a wonder, but he needed to learn discipline.

SHAYLA KERSTEN

Tomorrow wasn't going to be easy. If only Cavan could get through the interview without falling apart. Biton's thoughts sped around his mind, touching on all the possible outcomes. Too many things could go wrong, but the interview was necessary.

Sleep wasn't happening in spite of his exhaustion. Climbing out of the bed, he grabbed the robe hanging over the footboard then headed into the living room. Opening the window, he took a deep breath of the cool night air. His townhouse was in a quiet neighborhood, at least quiet for New York. Sounds of traffic were distant but so familiar Biton blocked it out. The soft footsteps behind him seemed loud compared to the sounds of the night.

Biton didn't turn, but continued staring out the window. "Cavan, you should be sleeping."

"I'm sorry, Master. Will you punish me?" His tone sounded almost hopeful.

"You want me to discipline you?" Biton turned to stare at him. After everything Cavan had lived through, his request stunned Biton.

"If you desire, Master."

"What do you desire?" Biton moved away from the window.

A shaft of light from the street lamp draped over Cavan. Dressed in sweatpants and a t-shirt, his arousal tented the front of his pants. He swallowed hard as his body shuddered.

"I ask you what you desired."

"To serve you, Master."

56

The idea of taking him was tempting. Biton's cock twitched at the memory of Cavan's mouth, at the tight heat of his ass. "How? Tell me how you want to serve me." Biton kept moving until his face was within inches of Cavan's.

The slender redhead seemed so much smaller, but in truth, he was only an inch or so shorter than Biton's six foot one frame.

"However you want." Cavan's panted words sent warm breath across Biton's lips.

"Do you enjoy pain?"

"I… I'm here to serve you."

"But do you enjoy it?" Biton needed to know. As much as he wanted to see Cavan's freckled ass bright with the red marks of a paddle or a lash, he wanted it to be because Cavan desired it.

"I… It doesn't matter, Master. Please use me…" The word choked off with a slight sob.

Slowly exhaling, Biton suppressed the intense urges rushing through his body. "Not tonight."

The severe disappointment in Cavan's eyes made his next decision easy.

He brought a hand up to caress Cavan's face. "No pain tonight." His fingers trailed across the stubble of a day old beard. "Tonight we try gentleness." Leaning in Biton nibbled at Cavan's soft lower lip.

Cavan's mouth opened against the gentle pressure though his hands still hung at his sides. Persistence paid off as the thin lips began to move.

Biton slipped an arm around his waist pulling him

close. The heat of Cavan's erection seeped through the sweatpants and Biton's robe. His own cock filled and lengthened with the exquisite pressure. "Hold me," he mumbled between kisses.

Cavan's hands moved to his hips and rested there. Fingers dug in and released.

Biton deepened the kiss from playful nips to crushing force as his tongue chased Cavan's into the warm depths.

Slowly, Cavan's hands slid around until his arms embraced Biton. His fingers pulled at the thin robe.

Need swelled in Biton as he pulled away from Cavan's mouth. "Come on." His arm around his lover's waist, he led him into the bedroom.

Determined to show Cavan the gentle side of lovemaking, he let the need to dominate slide off him with his robe. His boxer briefs did nothing to hide his arousal. With Erik, they hadn't always played games. Most of the time, their love life was like any other gay couple. Tonight, Biton would show Cavan how the other half lived. Until the younger man understood the difference, he couldn't make a choice.

Biton reached for Cavan's bowed head, his fingers gripped his chin and raised his face to Biton's gaze. The small lamp by the bed reflected the fear in the pale eyes.

"Don't be afraid. There'll be no pain tonight." Biton moved closer, his gaze held the frightened young man's. His words didn't seem to reassure. Maybe actions would.

His hands cupped the pale face as he drew closer. A

light kiss turned to a soft nibble. Hesitant still, Cavan's mouth responded. Biton pulled back and let his thumb run across the soft wet lower lip. "I want you naked," he whispered.

Cavan's hands moved to the hem of his t-shirt.

"No, I want to undress you."

His arms fell limp to his sides.

Biton's hands trailed from Cavan's face, down his chest and to his hips. A shiver ran through the slender body, but Biton didn't know if fear or desire or a combination of both were the cause. His lips met Cavan's again as his hands slid under the t-shirt. Soft skin, cool to the touch, enticed his fingers. A shudder ran through the lean body at his touch. "Are you cold?"

Almost undetectable, Cavan's head shook.

"Are you afraid?"

A slight nod.

"Don't be," Biton whispered against the soft lips. His hands slid up Cavan's body bunching the t-shirt as they moved. Leaning over, his tongue circled a tiny nipple. It pebbled and tightened at the attention.

Another shudder racked Cavan's slender frame.

"Do you like that?"

Cavan's hands clenched at his sides, but he didn't answer.

"Talk to me. Do you like this?" Biton suckled the other nipple.

"Yes…Master…" Panted breaths accompanied a slight moan.

His tongue circled the hardened nub once again

before he moved away. Cavan raised his arms as Biton pulled the t-shirt over his head and tossed it away. The pale skin glowed in the soft light of the lamp. Tugging at the slim hips until their bodies melded together from shoulder to groin, Biton then licked the curve of the tempting neck. The hardness of Cavan's erection rubbing against him sent searing heat through him. "You feel good." He nipped at the tight muscle in Cavan's shoulder as his hands slipped past the waist of the baggy sweats and grasped the tight ass. Kneading the firm flesh, Biton pulled him closer, increasing the pressure on his cock.

A soft moan accompanied the light flutter of fingers along Biton's waist.

"You can hold me, Cavan."

The hesitant hands slid around his waist then up Biton's bare back. Damp palms and splayed fingers rubbed his muscles with soft faltering movements.

Biton's hands circled around from Cavan's ass to his cock. Grasping the hot dripping flesh, Biton smiled at his lover's moan. "Did you like it when I sucked you?"

"Oh…yes…Master…"

Biton nuzzled Cavan's earlobe. "Do you want me to do it again?" His hand stoked the hard cock as he nibbled a trail from Cavan's ear to his neck.

"I…serve…"

"I asked what you wanted."

Cavan's fingers dug into Biton's back. "I want… what you want, Master," he panted.

"I want to kiss you all over, Cavan. I want to suck

60

your cock until you spill your come all over my tongue. Then I want to fuck you, hard and long, until you scream my name from the pleasure. Is that what you want?"

"Oh…oh…yes, Master."

Biton smiled against the nape of Cavan's neck. Releasing the hot weeping flesh, Biton slid the sweatpants down before he pushed Cavan toward the bed. He eased him down on the mattress then pulled the pants free of his ankles.

Sprawled before him, highlighted by the soft glow of the lamp, Cavan's pale flesh trembled. His cock, an angry red and weeping with desire, lay against his stomach. His lips parted, his tongue dashed out to moisten them as the pale green eyes tracked Biton's every move. Acceptance mingled with need replaced the earlier fear.

Biton welcomed the desire written across his features, proof Cavan wanted him and not just wanted to serve him.

Biton freed his dick from his boxers, pushed the tight material past his hips then kicked them off his feet.

Starting at Cavan's inner thigh, Biton kissed and licked a wet trail to the shaved balls. First mouthing the sac with gentle nips before his tongue teased the wrinkled texture. Biton looked up to see Cavan's head thrown back. His open mouth moved, but no sound came out.

"Talk to me, Cavan." He licked the length of hard

flesh. His tongue dipped into the wet slit. "I want to hear how you feel."

The only sound was a soft groan. Cavan's teeth bit into his lip muffling any words.

With slow easy movement, Biton kissed his way up the trembling man until he covered him with his body. As the heat of their erections collided, an electrical jolt of pleasure shot through him. His teeth nipped at Cavan's trapped lower lip until he released it. Biton soothed the bruised flesh with gentle suckling. Rocking slowly against Cavan's body, Biton whispered, "You can talk to me. Tell me anything. Right now, we're lovers, not master and slave. Tonight, I want to make you feel good."

Cavan pushed up against Biton. His body slid into sync as Biton's head dipped in for another kiss. Slow deep kisses, tongues tangling grew harder as their bodies met in an ever-faster dance. Cavan's hands moved to Biton's back pulling him tighter.

"Yes, Cavan, hold me." A hot hungry mouth muffled Biton's words.

Cavan's legs twined with his until they were tangled together.

"Yes…" Biton breathed.

Pre-come slicked their stomachs as Biton moved faster. All the other things he wanted to do slipped out the window, chased away by intense desire pooling in his groin. "Come for me, Cavan."

Within seconds, liquid heat splattered against his stomach. Cavan's legs tightened around him, hampering his movement, but it didn't matter. Sweet release poured from him to mix with his lover's juices. His mouth devoured Cavan's as he shuddered against the slender body until languid satisfaction filled him and sated exhaustion stilled him. Burying his face in Cavan's neck, Biton breathed a hopeful sigh. Tenderness for this lost soul already seeped through him.

With a soft groan, he forced his head up to look at his lover.

Cavan's open mouth panted hot breaths. His fingers traced his kiss-bruised lips.

"Are you okay?" Biton rose up on his elbows, easing some of his weight off Cavan.

"Yes, Master."

"Say my name." Shifting his weight to one arm, his hand grasped Cavan's fingers. Pulling them to his mouth, he kissed his knuckles. "Call me by my name."

His teeth worried his lower lip before he spoke. "Biton…"

———

Afraid to breathe, Cavan couldn't relax. His Master's arm wrapped around him was almost as terrifying as it was comforting. He shouldn't be afraid. His Master said things were different. The steady breathing and gentle heartbeat were reassuring. And he had fallen asleep with his Master earlier and hadn't gotten in trouble. The confusing difference to his old life cluttered his tired mind. His tongue snaked out and ran along his lips. His former Master never kissed him, no one had until

Master Biton. "Biton," he mouthed the word silently.

The memory of…Biton's body on his, the kisses, the pleasure… His breath caught in his throat. Could his life really be different? Maybe for thirty days. After that…

———

Biton hoped he appeared calm because he sure didn't feel it. A quick glance at the clock confirmed only five minutes passed since he last looked. Another half hour before Antonio and the cops arrived. Normally, Biton ate cops for breakfast. As a defense attorney, he knew the way they worked. He also knew the skeptical nature of anyone when dealing with BDSM. Wandering back to the kitchen for more coffee, he found Cavan still seated at the table.

Hunched over and dressed in sweats too big for him, he looked about fifteen. The blank, almost catatonic, expression on his face didn't bode well for the interview. Twice Cavan's nightmares woke Biton up during the night. He calmed down quickly, but both times insisted nothing was wrong.

Instead of refilling his cup, he set it in the sink. Cavan's body was so tense he looked as if he'd shatter when touched. Biton walked over and rested his hands on the younger man's shoulders. A slight flinch was the only recognition. "Cavan, you don't have to be so afraid."

"I… ah…" His breath quickened as he shuddered. "Master…"

Biton pulled the chair away from the table and knelt in front of the terrified man. "I'll be right here with you the whole time."

He looked like a wild creature caught in the headlights of a car, skittish and ready to run, but without knowing where to go. His tongue slipped out to wet his dry lips.

Unable to resist the temptation his moist lips presented, Biton leaned in for a gentle kiss. When he pulled away, the wild desperate look softened.

"Right here with you," he whispered as he laced his fingers through Cavan's.

They both jumped at the sound of a knock at the door.

"They're a little early. You ready?"

⎯⎯

"Come in." Biton motioned to Antonio and the stern looking man with him. At Biton's prompting, Cavan had moved to the living room. Biton kept his voice low so he wouldn't hear them in the foyer. "He's very nervous. I'm not sure this is going to work."

"It has to be done," Antonio whispered.

"I know. I just wanted to warn you."

"This is Detective Ramos with Special Victims. He knows how to handle situations like this."

Biton nodded at the introduction. "Biton Savakis." After shaking hands with the detective, he motioned both men toward the living room.

Antonio lagged behind, whispering, "Oh, Biton, I

brought Cavan's clothes from my place."

"Thanks. I plan to get him some more soon." Biton accepted the small bag Antonio offered.

When they entered the living room, they found Cavan folded up in a corner of the couch, his knees hugged tight to his chest.

Biton's heart ached at the sad picture the younger man presented. He dropped the bag beside the lamp table then walked over to Cavan and squeezed his shoulder. "It'll be okay," he whispered. "They're here to help. I want you to tell them everything about your foster parents and Wainwright; whatever they ask." Biton felt the trembling under his hand.

Cavan opened his mouth to answer, but words didn't form. Instead, he nodded his understanding.

"Have a seat, gentlemen." Biton motioned to the two armchairs opposite the couch.

Biton sat down next to Cavan, their shoulders touching. Maybe Cavan could gain some reassurance from the contact. Biton really wanted to wrap his arms around the tense body and tell him everything would be okay.

"Michael, I understand this is difficult for you, but we need information." Ramos kept his mellow baritone voice low and gentle.

At the sound of his real name, Cavan flinched.

Biton resisted the urge to tangle his fingers through the younger man's.

"Can you tell me the name of your last foster father?"

"Pa...Pablo." The stammered word was barely more than a whisper.

Ramos looked down to write on his note pad. "Do you remember his last name?"

Cavan's trembling started out slow, but soon his body shook so hard his teeth rattled. "I can't...I..." His words sputtered on shaky breath.

Afraid Cavan would pass out again, heedless of Ramos' watchful eyes, Biton slipped his arm around him, pulling him tight. "It's okay, Cavan. No one will hurt you. I promise. I'll keep you safe."

"Ma... Master..." Cavan turned to bury his face in Biton's neck. "I don't want to die... Not like Mateo... Please don't make me tell." The words tumbled out of Cavan in a flood of panic. "Please, Master."

Biton closed his eyes to the shocked look on the detectives face. He didn't know if it was because of Cavan's words about dying or the fact he called Biton Master. At the moment, he realized he didn't really care if Ramos knew his relationship to the terrified young man. He'd get over it. "Who's Mateo, Cavan?"

His face still buried in the crook of Biton's neck, the words were muffled. "My old Master's slave..."

Biton opened his eyes and met Ramos'. The detective nodded so Biton continued. "What happened to Mateo?" Biton kept his voice low.

"He was bad... The Master said he had to be punished."

"You mean Wainwright?"

"Yes." Cavan's arms moved around Biton.

"What did Wainwright do to him?"

"I can't tell!" His fingers dug into Biton's back as the panic in his voice escalated.

"You have to tell me, Cavan. Remember, I'm your Master now. You have to obey me." Biton's gaze stayed locked with Ramos' as he said the words. The hell with propriety. Cavan's wellbeing took priority. "What did Wainwright do to Mateo?"

Ramos nodded his approval.

"He beat him... So bad... So much blood... Please," Cavan's voice cracked, "please, Master, I don't want to die like that..."

"I won't punish you for telling the truth. That won't happen to you. I'll protect you. It's part of my responsibilities. Remember yesterday? We talked about this. I have the responsibility to care for you."

As terrified shaking racked the slender body, Cavan's fingers dug into Biton's back so hard, he knew he would have bruises.

"Gentlemen, would you excuse us a moment?" The sympathy in Ramos' eyes sent relief flooding through Biton. There could be repercussions later from his open admission, but for now...

Antonio stood and motioned for Ramos to follow him. "Come on. I know where he keeps the good coffee."

Biton smiled as his friend led the other officer into the kitchen. His attention quickly turned back to Cavan. "It's okay. I've got you and nothing is going to happen to you for telling the truth." He rocked the hysterical man gently as he kissed the side of his face.

"It hurt so much when he whipped me. I thought… I was sure… I didn't want to die like Mateo."

Threading his fingers through Cavan's hair, he tugged gently until the red-rimmed eyes met his gaze. "I won't let anything like that happen to you. Antonio and the other officer will make sure Wainwright won't do it to anyone else. But you have to tell them everything. We have to stop him. Do you understand how important this is? Do you have any idea how wrong Wainwright was?"

Although still panting, most of Cavan's tears subsided. "He was the Master. He said he could do anything he wanted to his slaves."

"He was wrong. Just because someone pledges his life to a master doesn't entitle the Master to seriously injure or kill. Remember what I said yesterday, about a contract?"

Cavan nodded slowly.

"I told you I was responsible for your health. That means I don't do anything that could really hurt you. Playing sexual games is supposed to be good for both of us. Pain, inflicted with care to someone willing, is meant to bring about eventual pleasure. Even if you've agreed to be my slave, you have the right to tell me when it's too much to handle. You have the *obligation* to tell me." Biton leaned forward and brushed a kiss against Cavan's lips. "If I went too far, if I hurt you too much, I wouldn't be holding up my end of the contract. You have to understand that if this," Biton tapped Cavan's chest and then his own, "between us is going to work."

Cavan nodded slightly, but the confusion in his eyes remained.

"You have to finish telling them what happened, to you and to Mateo and anyone else your foster father and Wainwright hurt. Can you do this?"

"Yes, Master…" Cavan's eyes grew wide with fear. "I'm sorry! I… I…"

"What's wrong?"

"I wasn't supposed to call you Master." The relative calm from only a minute ago fled.

"No, you weren't. But we'll discuss that later, after our guests leave. Now you have to talk to them again." His stern tone seemed to reassure Cavan.

The man was full of contradictions and misguided notions. Retraining was going to be a long road and one Biton wouldn't be able to do alone.

———

Cavan watched his Master walk toward the kitchen. The uncontrollable fear still bubbled through his gut like a deep hunger. Master had promised to protect him and he should believe him, but he couldn't. He would tell the men what they wanted to know. He had to. His Master said so.

Resignation flowed through him, quelling the fear. Master made him feel so good. His touch, his kisses, even his cock in him, so different from before, so wonderful. If Master Biton wanted him to tell, he would, regardless of the consequences. For thirty days with him, he would suffer whatever happened later.

Chapter Five

Biton took a deep breath and exhaled slowly as he walked toward the kitchen. The revelation of the nature of their relationship was inevitable. He should have known Cavan would react the way he did. It was almost a relief. Watching Cavan's fear and not being able to comfort him was too difficult.

A slight smile twitched his lips. In such a short time, he'd become very fond of the sad redhead. Or maybe having someone to take care of again made his life worth living.

The detectives looked up expectantly when he walked into the kitchen.

"Gentlemen, let's try this again. He's still upset, but I think he has very good reason to be. It appears Wainwright has done more than just abuse his slaves."

Antonio spoke first. "Did he say Mateo died?"

"No, but it sounds like it. He's ready to talk again.

I think." Biton scrubbed his face with the heel of his palms. "Cavan has been through extreme torture and God knows what else. He may be twenty-five, but emotionally he's not much more than a teenager. I don't think he's ever been shown affection or love and doesn't know how to handle it."

Looking at Detective Ramos, Biton continued, "My relationship with him is something I'd prefer not spread around. You should be able to understand that. I want you to know I wouldn't hurt him, not like what he's suffered. He never got the chance to choose this lifestyle. But right now, he doesn't understand any other way. I promised to take care of him and I plan to get him psychological help."

"Mr. Savakis, you have to realize I've seen about every sexual perver..." Ramos stopped and a slight flush rose on his neck. "I'm sorry. I may not understand your lifestyle, but this isn't the first time I've dealt with it. As far as I can see, you are trying to do the right thing with Mr. Delany. The only thing that needs to go in our report is his statement."

"Thank you." Biton turned to head toward the door then turned back. "Oh, and about his name. Calling him Cavan might ease his discomfort. Yesterday, when I made him tell me his real name, he hyperventilated and passed out. Confirm it for your notes, but then call him Cavan."

"Good idea," Ramos nodded.

When they returned to the living room, Cavan hadn't moved from his spot in the corner of the couch.

Biton didn't hesitate this time. He took his seat next to him, slid his arm around his shoulders then pulled him tight against him. The fingers of his free hand threaded through Cavan's.

Ramos pulled the armchair closer to the couch and sat down. "Cavan, I really need to know what happened to you and Mateo. I know a little bit. How about I tell you what I know and you tell me if it's right or not?"

Biton nodded at Ramos' new approach. Treating Cavan more as a child than an adult might work.

Cavan nodded slightly as his fingers tightened on Biton's hand.

"Good, good, Cavan. Now, Biton says you're real name is Michael Delany. Is that true?"

"Yes, sir," was the barely whispered answer.

"Very good." Ramos' broad smile seemed to calm Cavan. "We looked you up in the foster care system. It says you ran away from the Stevens family when you were eleven. Did you?"

Biton watched Cavan carefully.

With a slight frown wrinkling his forehead, he shook his head. "No, sir. I… I…" He turned to look at Biton. "I wouldn't do that. I wouldn't run away." His panted breath was hot against Biton's face.

"Shhh…" Biton leaned in, letting his forehead touch Cavan's. "I know you wouldn't. We just need to figure out why they thought you did."

Cavan's eyes closed and his breathing slowed again.

"Cavan," Ramos reached out and touched Cavan's arm. "If you didn't run away from the Stevens', where did you go?"

"They moved me. My next foster family, the Smith's."

Ramos met Biton's gaze. "The Smiths. Do you remember where or what school you went to?"

Cavan shook his head. "I didn't go to school when I lived there. They said I was finished. I didn't understand that, but it was okay. They weren't mean to me."

"Were they the ones who sold you? To Wainwright?"

"No…" Cavan ducked his chin onto his chest. "My… It was… After them. The next family."

Biton closed his eyes against the prickly sting of tears. As a person who wanted complete control in his life, Biton couldn't imagine the horror Cavan had endured from childhood until now. It made him sick to his stomach, but even more, it made his heart ache for the lost young man fiercely gripping his hand.

———

Biton tucked his exhausted lover into the bed. The interview lasted well into the afternoon and didn't garner much information. Running his hand through the short red hair, Biton smiled at the sleepy eyes watching him. "You did very good, Cavan, very good. I'm proud of you."

Tears welled up making the green eyes greener, like grass after a summer rain.

"Sleep now. I'll be back later. I need to talk to Antonio and Detective Ramos." He leaned in for a swift kiss, but Cavan's hand slid up around his neck, briefly keeping him there. Biton deepened the kiss, his tongue slipping between the parted lips. Cavan's tongue chased his when he pulled away. The simple act encouraged Biton. With a final gentle nip to Cavan's lips, he whispered, "I'll be back in a little bit."

With a long sigh, Cavan's eyes closed and his breathing steadied.

Biton hated to leave him. He was determined to see his guests out as quickly as possible and return. He was afraid the interview would bring out Cavan's nightmares. Moving to the open door, he eased it closed on his way out.

Antonio and Ramos were talking quietly in the living room. They looked up as he came back into the room.

"We have enough to arrest Wainwright for assault and battery, but we need to know more about the murder," Antonio said.

Cavan hadn't been able to tell them what happened to Mateo after the beating. Biton shuddered at the memory of Cavan's monotone voice as he related the bloody scene. Wainwright literally flayed his slave with a cat-o-nine-tails whip. Cavan thought Mateo was still alive when he and three other slaves were ushered out of the room. As a warning, they had been forced to watch the punishment. No wonder Wainwright terrified Cavan. Then when he received similar punishment last winter, he was sure he would die.

"Well, without a body, there's no evidence of a murder." Biton wanted to shove the lawyer in him out the door and face Wainwright as a man with vengeance in mind.

"I know." Antonio sighed. "If I'd only…"

Biton could read his thoughts. They'd known months ago what Cavan had suffered. The hospital reports would be part of the evidence. Cavan gave permission to release them earlier. Unfortunately, how many others had suffered, or died, in the last three months was unknown. "Well, Cavan's statement should get a search warrant. Maybe we'll find evidence of Mateo's fate. In the meantime, I'll talk to Cavan some more. Maybe he'll remember more when he calms down."

The interrogation had been extremely tough on Cavan. By the end, he was covered in sweat and tears and exhausted. When the state listed him as a runaway, he had moved in with another family, who he lived with for a year and a half. They hadn't harmed him. He had been treated as a menial servant: cleaning and cooking; but no sexual abuse. And evidently browbeating his self-confidence and self-esteem.

"It looks like the first 'off the books' family was preparing him for future slavery." Biton said as he walked toward his liquor cabinet. Holding up a bottle of scotch, he looked at Antonio and Ramos. Both men shook their head. "On duty, huh? Well, I'm not." He splashed some into a glass and tossed it back. The fiery liquid burned through his veins as hot as his anger with Wainwright.

"Yeah," Antonio sighed and rubbed his eyes with

his fingers. "The first family would muddy the trail. If someone found where Cavan was, they hadn't really done anything to him except keep him out of school. Since no one ever came around, they were able to pass him on to the next family to continue his training."

Ramos drew a long breath and stood. "We have a bigger problem than just Cavan and a few others. It's too efficient, too long term. As much as I hate the idea, we have a very organized slave trading operation going on here. No telling how many kids have been pushed through this system and into God knows what. I have to get back to the office." A frown creased his brow. "We're going to need to check out every runaway listed with Child Services for who knows how long. Cavan's ordeal started fourteen years ago. With thousands of children in the system, we could be talking hundreds of victims."

Biton had already thought of it, but the horror on Antonio's face proved he hadn't.

"My God…" Antonio's face paled under his naturally dark complexion. "I…"

Ramos slapped him on the back as he headed for the door. "That's homicide detectives for you. Your focus is too narrow. Come on. We need to get out of here." He continued toward the door.

Biton walked them out. "Thank you for being so gentle with Cavan."

"It's not the first time I've seen a case like this. He needs professional help and a chance to live a normal life."

Ramos didn't have to say it.

Biton nodded. "I know. I will make an appointment with a psychiatrist as soon as possible. And he will have a choice. I know you don't understand my lifestyle, but believe me when I tell you I want a willing partner not a mindless slave."

Ramos nodded and offered his hand. "I will do everything I can to be discreet."

Biton shook the outstretched hand. "Thank you." He watched as the two men walked down the stairs and out of the building.

More than anything Biton wanted a willing, consensual relationship. And it surprised him to realize how much he wanted it with his temporary redheaded slave.

———

Cavan fought the hands holding him as fear spiked through him. The warm cocoon of blankets turned to rough leather straps holding him. The soft sheets morphed into the sting of the cat against his back.

"No, please, no!" Shouting hadn't done any good then. Begging for his life only made the Master madder. The sharp smell of blood mixed with the acrid smell of sweat. "No!"

"Cavan, wake up! Come on. You're safe. No one will hurt you here. Can you hear me, Cavan?"

"Master." Relief washed through him as strong arms pulled him close. His head rested on the muscled chest. A thin layer of cloth separated him from the rapid sound of Master Biton's heart.

"You're okay. I won't let anything happen to you." His master's arms were tight as he rocked him. "You were very good today."

The praise caused a lump in Cavan's throat and a warm rush flow through him.

"I needed to know about your life as much as the police did. It changes things...the way you've been treated..."

His happiness dissipated in a flood of panic. "Changes? But you said I was good."

"You were. And you did, are doing, the right thing by making sure Wainwright and your foster parents never hurt anyone else." His Master paused to plant a soft kiss on his head. "But you didn't choose this life, Cavan. Being a submissive should be your decision, not something forced on you. Your childhood stolen from you, you were abused and raped. All these things are wrong and the people who did it must go to jail." Another soft kiss accompanied a gentle sigh. "Who knows if you would have chosen a man as a lover if you'd been given a choice?"

"I want to stay with you..." Cavan couldn't stop the tight-throated panic. "I just..."

"Shhhh... You will stay with me for now; until you can make a decision about what you want."

"I want you."

"You say that now, but you need to wait until you've had a chance to learn the difference between a choice and something forced on you."

"I want to stay with you, Master." He wasn't being sent away. If his Master said he had a choice, his decision was made. He wanted to stay with his new Master. The terror began to recede. He would stay. No matter what happened, as long as his Master wanted him, he would stay.

———

Biton relaxed as Cavan's breathing leveled off into sleep. He was sure the younger man still didn't understand what he was saying. The idea of his leaving already sent pain through his heart. How could he have fallen so hard, so fast? His feelings didn't matter though. Tomorrow, they would start fresh. Instead of retraining Cavan to be a proper submissive for him, he would help him become an independent person first.

———

A warm hand surrounded his cock. Long lazy strokes pulled Biton from sleep. Morning light showed through the curtains. Fast breathing shook the body plastered against him whether from fear or desire, he didn't know.

"Cavan?"

"Yes, Master." A tremor of fear tinged the quiet response.

"You feel good." He tightened his arm around the slender body. "Really good." Biton wanted to roll Cavan over and plow his body until waves of pleasure washed through him. But the decision made last night

81

stopped him. "Cavan, why are you stroking me?"

"I should stop?" Confusion colored his voice.

Biton wasn't sure where to start and the pleasure of Cavan's strokes fusing his synapses wasn't helping. Start with the basics. "Do you enjoy being with a man?"

"I… I do with you." The warm hand faltered.

Biton slid his hand under the cover and wrapped around Cavan's. "I haven't always known I was gay." He held tight, stilling the sensuous motions. "Until I was twenty-two, I tried to convince myself I wanted women, until my first male lover. The revelation was almost more mind blowing than the sex." Biton shivered at the memory. "It wasn't sweet and tender, it was hard and rough and I couldn't get enough. The relationship didn't last long, but I knew a woman would never satisfy me the way a man did. Before we parted ways, I had discovered my need to control my partner and the desire for that partner to be a man. But both were my choice."

Sliding his fingers around Cavan's wrist, he pulled the man's hand away from his cock. Rolling toward him, Biton caressed the stubble roughened face. "You never had the chance to make that choice. How can you know if what you feel for me is desire or gratitude for giving you a safe place to stay? Or is it a sense of obedience because you've never known another way of life?"

"I want you. I want to stay with you." Panic made Cavan's voice tight and his eyes wild.

"Why?" Biton whispered. "If you had the chance to

leave here, a place to live without obligation to anyone but yourself, would you take it?"

"I…" A half-choked sob swallowed the rest of his words.

"I'm not saying you have to leave. If you stay, it should be because you want this life and not because you have no choice." Biton ran his thumb across the trembling bottom lip. He leaned and brushed a kiss against the sorrowful line of Cavan's mouth. "You have to tell me what you want."

Cavan's neck strained forward, chasing Biton's mouth until he caught it. "Please…" he mumbled against Biton's lips.

Biton melted into a gentle kiss. He ached with need, but his desire had to be tempered. And the feeling of tenderness had to be quelled before it became something deeper. If Cavan didn't accept the life of a submissive willingly, Biton would lose him. The idea made his breath catch in his throat. As the tempting lips pressed against his opened mouth, Biton couldn't stop himself from falling in.

His fingers splayed against Cavan's face as his body moved closer. The heat of Cavan's mouth couldn't compare to the hot cock pressed against Biton through thin layers of cotton. That Cavan desired him wasn't in question. But why? Because Biton was gentle where others were cruel? Would Biton ever know his real feelings?

Desire pushed away the nagging questions. Sucking the shy tongue teasing his mouth, Biton pulled Cavan closer. The slender body melted against him. Biton's fingers raked the short red hair. The ache in his groin intensified to scorching heat.

"Want you…" Cavan moaned as he gasped for breath.

The desperate desire to push into the velvet heat of Cavan's tight ass almost overwhelmed him. "Cavan…" Biton wanted to tell him no, but the desperate hands pulling at him stilled his protests and dissolved his thoughts.

Holding him close, Biton rolled their bodies until Cavan was pinned beneath him. The frantic pace of their kisses slowed. Biton stroked the short hair as he pulled away from Cavan's mouth.

The pale green eyes held such trust, such innocence. How could he, after all he'd been through, trust anyone?

Could Biton give up the part of his being that craved the control of his partner? Would he leave behind the pleasure of pain to keep the trust and innocence lighting Cavan's eyes?

With a sigh, he dipped his head to nuzzle Cavan's ear. A soft moan tickled his jaw. As reward for a nibbled ear lobe, Cavan's hips surged up. His legs scrabbled for purchase around Biton's pulling them tighter together. The exquisite pressure of cock against cock caused Biton a few moans of his own.

Mouthing a wet trail back to Cavan's lips, Biton inhaled his whimper of desire as his tongue sought out the moist cavern. Teeth clashed as he sought deeper contact.

Cavan's mouth responded with matching hunger and desperate hands clawed at his neck, holding them together.

"God, I want you so bad," Biton groaned when he came up for air. "I need…"

"Take me, Master…" Cavan's breath panted across his face. "Please take me…"

Biton shuddered at the pleading sound of his voice. He needed this, someone begging him for relief and release. Pulling away, he reached for the nightstand. Snagging a condom and lube, he dropped them next to Cavan. With calm slow breaths, he reigned in some of his desire as he knelt between the long legs and reached for Cavan's shorts.

Cavan lifted his hips and pushed the material down as Biton pulled. The shorts flew over Biton's shoulder in his haste. Cavan's already leaking cock was too tempting. He leaned forward and swallowed the hot flesh with a greedy mouth, pushing until the tip reached deep in his throat. Cavan's body arched, almost gagging Biton with the sudden movement.

"Master!" Fear tinged the cry as much as desire.

Biton used his mouth to reassure Cavan. Pulling away until he suckled the head, he glanced up at the tense body. Fear faded and trust resurrected as Biton ran his tongue around the hard ridge of the crown. His fingers rolled the soft sac of Cavan's balls before searching down the crack of his ass to tease the puckered object of his needs.

With a final swipe of his tongue, Biton pulled away

85

from his lover's swollen flesh. "Turn over."

Cavan didn't hesitate, scrambling over onto his hands and knees, exposed for Biton's whim. Framed by his open thighs, his hard cock hung heavy, balls tight with need.

Presented with the sweet tight ass, Biton fought with impatient desire. As much as he wanted to take him hard and fast, he wouldn't. He shouldn't be taking advantage of Cavan in the first place, but he needed him so much his body spiked with sharp pain.

Biton bent over Cavan and licked a trail down the arched spine. His throat tightened as he kissed the thick scarring that crisscrossed Cavan's back. His hands caressed ribs and stomach as they slid toward the hard flesh.

Long slow pulls on Cavan's shaft made the younger man moan, but he never voiced his desire.

"Tell me what you want, Cavan." Biton rubbed his own aching cock in the cleft of Cavan's ass. "What do you want?"

"You…" Cavan pushed his ass against Biton as he moaned the word.

"Tell me what you want and I'll do it." Biton leaned over until his chest rested along Cavan's back. Kissing his neck, he whispered, "Tell me what to do with you." So many meanings in his words.

"Oh… Master…fuck…me…" His words kept time with Biton's long hard strokes on Cavan's cock.

Biton pulled away then kissed a gentle path down Cavan's back until he reached the tempting ass. His tongue teased the dimple at the cleft of his cheeks. Releasing Cavan's cock, Biton used both hands to spread the milky mounds apart. The dusky puckered rose almost pulsed with need. He ran his tongue through the valley and down, teasing the tight hole. Circling it with the tip of his tongue first, he then laved the hole.

Cavan moaned as his head settled on the bed, his fingers twisting in the covers. "Master!"

Biton slid his hand between Cavan's thighs and stroked the heated shaft of flesh. His tongue poked and prodded the tight pucker as it began to relax and open. Lubricated by an almost constant flow of pre-come, Cavan's hot cock slid easily though his hand. Biton rolled his tongue and pushed against Cavan's loosened hole.

A whimpered groan and a push against Biton's face preceded Cavan's spurting climax. Biton pulled the leaking cock back and sucked the hot flesh into his mouth. Cavan buried his face in the covers and moaned as Biton sucked him dry. As soon as he released him, Cavan's body slid down on to the mattress.

Biton hurt with need as he grabbed the lube. With slick fingers, he quickly prepared Cavan's ass, pushing lube deep into the already relaxed hole. Tearing open a condom, he rolled it down his aching flesh and slicked lube on with a few quick strokes. With Cavan sprawled flat on the bed, he pushed into the velvet heat. "Gentle... Must..." A slight push from Cavan and Biton was balls deep in molten heat.

"Oh, yes… Cavan…" Biton leaned forward, lowering his body he covered his lover. Slow rolling movements kept him close to the edge. A flurry of kisses and teasing bites showered Cavan's neck and shoulder. Sucking his earlobe, Biton murmured, "So good… So tight…" His arms curled under Cavan' chest as his body undulated on him, his cock enveloped in the intense heat. The knot in his groin tightened until he couldn't hold back anymore. With a sharp jab of his hips and an unintelligible cry, he fell over the edge and emptied into his lover.

With his limbs heavy and his heartbeat so fast he thought his heart would drill through his chest, the tremors of his climax continued to shudder through him. Several seconds passed before he realized he wasn't the only one shaking. Gentle muffled sobs from Cavan roused him from his languid bliss. "Cavan?" He rolled off the limp body. Stripping the condom off his cock, he tossed it in the trash before pulling Cavan close. "Did I hurt you?"

Cavan shook his head, but the tears streaming down his face didn't help convince Biton of his truthfulness. Biton didn't bother to ask again. Instead, he pulled him close, yanked the covers over them and held him, kissing the tears away.

———

Cavan woke alone and immediately missed the heat of his Master's body. A shiver ran through him when he thought about last night. His old master had used him often, had let his friends use him, but no one had ever touched him like Master Biton. His brain couldn't quite wrap itself around the whole experience. All the times he'd been required to rim someone, he never questioned. It was a slave's place to obey. The memory of his Master's hot tongue prodding his ass made his cock take notice. Why would his Master do something only fit for a slave?

The sound of movement in the other room reminded him of his place. A slave shouldn't be lounging in his master's bed. But then, Master Biton said things were different here. His old master's rules didn't apply. The sheer pleasure the man gave him should tell him that much, but still... He rolled out of the bed, happier than he ever remembered. A wave of panic swept through him. He shouldn't get used to it. Only thirty days and two of them were gone.

Chapter Six

"Harry, I'm sorry to call you at home, but I won't be in the office this week." Biton paced the dining room as he spoke to his law partner. "Something's come up."

"Biton, I know you've been having a difficult time since Erik's death, but the Hargrave deposition is this week."

The irritation in Harry's voice made Biton wince. He'd forgotten all about the case. "Okay, I'll be in for that on Tuesday." He should come clean. The Wainwright investigation was likely to move fast. "There's also some stuff you should know about. Some things maybe not so favorable to the firm."

"What's up?" Concern colored over the irritation.

"Maybe we should talk in person."

"Want to meet for coffee or at the office?"

"Why don't you come here?" Biton didn't really

want to leave Cavan alone. That was the whole reason he wanted time off.

"Okay, what time?"

"Now is fine. I've got someone I want you to meet anyway." Biton trusted Harry. They'd known each other since law school and Harry knew everything about him.

"Someone?" Harry's voice teased.

"Yeah, someone." Biton turned to see a pale faced Cavan. "I've got to go. I'll see you in a little while, okay?"

"Sure thing."

Biton turned off the phone before Harry could say anything else. He walked over to Cavan. The pale face worried him. "Do you feel okay? You don't look too good."

"I'm fine, Master." A slight quiver in his voice wasn't very convincing.

"Are you hungry? You didn't eat last night."

Cavan had been so exhausted he slept through without waking yesterday. Then he went back to sleep after they made love this morning. He should look rested.

"No, Master."

"Why don't you go lay back down for a little while? I have a business associate coming over in a little while."

"Yes, Master."

Biton watched Cavan as he almost stumbled for the bedroom. Something wasn't right with him, but Biton didn't have time to pursue it. Harry only lived a few miles away. It wouldn't take him long to get here. He'd have to talk to Cavan later.

———

The coffee just finished brewing when Biton heard the doorbell. Harry must have dashed out of his house as soon as he hung up the phone. Of course, Biton was a little cryptic about possible trouble for the firm. With a glance at the closed bedroom door, he headed over to let his friend in.

"Thanks for coming," Biton said as he shook Harry's hand.

"Well, you have me curious. More for your new friend than any worry for the firm."

"They're related." Biton shut the door before motioning for Harry to precede him into the kitchen. "Coffee?"

"Sure," Harry said as he took a seat at the table. "So where's your friend?"

"Sleeping." Biton poured two cups of coffee and brought them to the table. He pushed a sugar bowl toward Harry.

Dipping a spoon into the sugar bowl, Harry smiled. "Erik's room or…"

Biton laughed at his friend's nosiness. "My room; thank you for asking." Harry had been one of the first people he'd come out to and the only one in the firm who knew the truth about his lifestyle.

"So besides finding a new *friend*, what's up?"

"Cavan, that's his name, or at least what he's called,

carries quite a bit of baggage and I want to help him. The repercussions to the firm could make it better for me to retire, or at least take a leave of absence."

"You're going to have to explain that a little more."

Biton sipped at his coffee before continuing. "He's been badly abused. Tortured in a way no one in my circle would ever do. And it's been going on since he was a teenager. Antonio and a Special Victims officer were over here yesterday. There'll be an investigation and it's likely to get a lot of publicity. You know how this city is."

"Ah yes, lurid details. The more the merrier."

"Detective Ramos is afraid it's a ring of pedophiles snatching kids from the foster care system. They list them as runaways and keep them out of school until they drop off the radar. Then they train them as sex slaves and sell them."

"Oh, my God!" Horror paled Harry's face.

"Yeah… Cavan was snatched at eleven and started his slavery by the time he was thirteen. We haven't exactly narrowed down when he was first sexually abused, but definitely before he was sixteen." Biton stared into his coffee cup. "I have to do what I can to make sure it's stopped."

"Of course you do! Though I don't see why you feel you have to leave the firm to do it."

Biton squirmed in his chair a little. "I've become… attached to him. He needs help, psychological and emotional. I won't desert him now, but if the details become public, I may not be able to hide our relationship."

"So?"

Biton set down his coffee cup and stood up. "He doesn't understand that being a slave is a lifestyle choice. He's never really known any other life. He thinks being tortured is normal." Biton paced the kitchen, anger at the people who did this to Cavan growing with each step. "He's a gentle soul. I don't think he'd be into submission if he hadn't been forced into it."

"And you want to keep him around." It wasn't a question and Harry hit the nail on the head.

Biton wanted Cavan, but the idea of giving up the thrill of control, of power over a helpless body, bound and gagged, waiting for his whim... The memory of Cavan strapped in the sling Friday made him shiver. "Yes."

The admission released the tension that nagged at him since yesterday. Was it really the idea of publicity and notoriety that scared him? Or was it the idea of losing him?

"Can I meet him?" Harry's voice startled him.

"Uh, yeah, I'll see if he's awake."

His mind mulled over the revelation as he walked to the bedroom. He wanted Cavan to stay, more than just thirty days. Cavan's sweet submissive nature appealed to his dominant streak. Part of him believed Cavan would never be an aggressive person. With his formative years spent subjugating any trace of self-confidence, it would take years of counseling to overcome even a small part of the damage done.

Could Biton give up the rougher side of his sex life to keep Cavan with him? Standing in front of the bedroom door, Biton paused. Making love to Cavan this morning had been exquisite. It still might not work, but it gave Biton a small degree of hope.

"Cavan," he said as he knocked. The sight before him when he opened the door made his jaw drop and his cock twitch.

Naked and sprawled spread eagle across the bed, Cavan waited. With a pale face and a limp cock, Cavan's eyes followed him into the room.

Even though Harry couldn't see into the bedroom, Biton closed the door quickly. "What are you doing?" He didn't mean to sound so harsh, but Cavan's obviously posed body startled him.

"Waiting for you…and your friend…" Tears still stained his face.

"Oh… no… Cavan." Biton's voice dropped to a gentle murmur as he climbed on the bed. "You aren't…" He pulled a tense and almost resisting body close and swallowed against the lump in his throat. "I don't share, Cavan. As long as you're mine, I won't let anyone else have you."

"But…" A sob choked off more words.

"I didn't bring Harry here for you to service. He's my friend and one of the partners in my law firm. I brought him here to talk to him about me taking some time off. And I needed to tell him about you before anyone finds out about the investigation."

"So I don't have to…"

"No, never." Biton kissed the top of his head. "Like I said, I don't share."

The tension flowed out of Cavan with racking sobs. His body curled around Biton like a blanket.

Rocking him gently, Biton realized where the stricken look earlier came from. Cavan must have overheard him on the phone with Harry. When he told him a friend was coming over, Cavan's face had been sheet white. Biton should have realized what that would have meant to Cavan.

"You're mine, Cavan," he whispered. And he wanted him to stay that way.

"Cavan," Biton yelled. "I'm going now." As much as he hated leaving him alone, Biton had no choice. The Hargrave case was too important for him to miss the deposition. Unfortunately, Antonio was on duty and Lia wouldn't get off her shift at the hospital until three this afternoon.

Biton turned around to see Cavan hovering in the doorway of the kitchen. After the internal revelation of his feelings for Cavan on Sunday, Biton spent most of yesterday showing Cavan how things worked in the apartment. He wanted him to feel comfortable here. When Cavan finally did make a choice, Biton wanted it to be to stay. If he felt at home, it would be easier.

It still amazed him the things Cavan didn't know, working a TV remote or making a telephone call seemed new to him. He could read, but at a grade school level.

Biton made a note to pick up some easier reading material.

He also took the time to write up the promised contract. Cavan was willing to sign it without looking, but Biton made him read it aloud, explaining everything in the agreement in detail. Even though he couched the terms as simple as possible, Cavan had difficulty with many of the words. Since he hadn't had access to reading material in more years than Biton cared to imagine, his reading skills were very rusty.

He also made Cavan sign his real name although he had to spell it for him. One of the items on his list of things to do was tutor him.

"I'm only going to be a little while," Biton said. "Come here." He held out his arms and Cavan moved into them. "I showed you how to use the remote, so watch TV." Holding him tight, Biton kissed his neck. "I won't be long. Don't leave the house and keep the doors locked." Pulling back so he could see Cavan's face, he smiled. "Okay?"

Cavan nodded but still didn't speak.

Maybe this wasn't a good idea, but Biton had little choice. A quick kiss and Biton released him. "I'll see you later."

It took all the willpower he could muster to walk out and lock the door behind him.

———

The deposition went smoothly, but the next appointment wouldn't be so easy. Biton opened the door to Dr. Merten's office hoping his nervousness didn't show.

Elizabeth Merten was a clinical psychiatrist. Often an expert witness for the prosecution, she had a reputation for treating the worst sexual abuse cases and her credentials were excellent. Although Biton laid out the basics of Cavan's life over the phone, she insisted they meet in person before she would agree to take him on as a patient.

The waiting area was elegant and calming with subtle earth tones. The receptionist, a perky young blonde, smiled as he entered the room.

"Can I help you, sir?"

"I'm Biton Savakis. I have an appointment with Dr. Merten."

"If you'll take a seat, I'll let her know you're here."

"Thank you." Biton walked over to a painting of a landscape and pretended fascination with it. He was too nervous to sit. He rarely spoke of his lifestyle outside the normal boundary of the local clubs. In the last few days, more people found out about his penchant for dominance and submission than he cared to have happen. Now yet another person wanted to ask questions.

"Mr. Biton, please come in."

Biton turned to see the dark haired Doctor standing in the door of her office. Her ample round figure didn't detract from her beauty. A warm smile framed by high cheekbones and an aristocratic nose influenced jurors as much as her credentials. People seemed to trust her almost immediately. Definitely a plus in her business and one of the reasons Biton called her. Cavan required special care.

"Thank you for seeing me on such short notice." Biton shook her hand before he took a seat in a comfortable easy chair. The décor of her office matched the calming waiting room.

"Cavan's case sounds difficult and I'm always up for a challenge." She sat in the matching chair facing Biton instead of behind her desk. She picked up a pad from a small table nearby. "I've already made some extensive notes from what you told me over the phone."

When they spoke yesterday, Biton told her everything he knew about Cavan's abduction and his life until three months ago. "Whatever you need to know; I want to help him."

Dr. Merten worried her upper lip with her teeth briefly then nodded. "Okay, then I need to know about your relationship with him. Keep in mind, anything said I will keep confidential though it's not strictly doctor-patient confidentiality."

Her words made him a little uncomfortable, but he wanted what was best for Cavan. "Okay," he said slowly.

"Good." She set pen to paper. "Are you having sexual relations with Cavan?"

"Uh…" Biton should have known better than to be shocked at her directness. From dealing with her through the prosecutor's office, he already knew she was forthright.

"Look, you told me he had been sexually abused by a cruel dominant. With the exception of his brief stay with a friend of yours, the last ten to twelve years have trained him to sexually service the man caring for him."

"You can't call what Wainwright did to him 'caring'." Biton riled at the idea of being compared to that freak. "I don't abuse him."

"But you said yourself he hadn't made a conscious choice to be submissive or even gay. He expects you to have sex with him." She raised her eyebrow as if waiting for him to challenge her statement. "He doesn't understand any other way."

"But I've never hurt him."

"Doesn't matter. If his therapy is going to work, you have to cease relations with him."

"He has to stay with me." A sudden lump in his throat made breathing difficult. "He has nowhere else to go, not where he'd be safe."

"I understand that," her voice gentled. "And I applaud your willingness to take care of him but the sex has to stop."

"He won't understand why." Trying to explain this to Cavan would be difficult. Even more, Biton didn't want him to have to sleep alone. Several times in the last few days, Cavan woke with nightmares, terrifying visions that left him covered in cold sweat and warm tears. Curling into Biton, he had calmed quickly. If he had to sleep alone, Biton knew he wouldn't come to him for comfort. He wouldn't disturb his master intentionally.

"And I'd prefer you don't tell him I suggested it." Her words derailed his train of thought.

"Suggested it?" A snort of ironic laughter escaped. "That didn't sound like a suggestion."

"You know what I mean. If you tell him it was my idea, it could prejudice him against me and that wouldn't be good for his therapy."

A sense of uneasiness settled in Biton's stomach. The last few days his world had centered on wiping the sadness from Cavan's eyes.

"Do you understand what I'm trying to say?"

"Yes," he sighed. "I do, but he…" Biton rubbed his eyes with his fingers. "I just want him to be happy."

"Hopefully, someday he will be. But first he needs to heal."

"Okay…" It wouldn't be easy, but somewhere during the last few days, Cavan's happiness became the most important thing in Biton's world.

———

Cavan tried to keep his breathing steady. His Master said he could do what he wanted, watch TV or read. The idea made his stomach churn with fear. Before… In his old life, touching things earned him a beating. Usually, when his Master didn't require his services, he had been locked in his tiny room. With nothing, but a pallet on the floor, Cavan would spend hours blanking out the world around him. At first, he dreamed about being rescued, a shadowy figure, maybe his real mother or father, coming into the cold cell and taking him away. But as he grew older, the fantasy hurt too much so he learned to tune out everything: the bare walls, the cold hard floor and most of all his Master's actions.

Now, free to roam Master Biton's apartment, with permission to do what he wanted, fear increased his breathing and made his heart race. Some part of his mind screamed it was a trick or a trap. What if this was a test? What would happen if he failed?

The memory of the lash peeling the skin from his back made him gasp for air. The crack of the whip and the copper smell of his own blood filled his senses. His mind tried to tell him it was over, that that old life was behind him, but the vivid memory couldn't be banished. Stumbling to his Master's room, Cavan crawled into the closet. Maybe the darkness would hide him from the demons.

———

"Cavan, I'm back." Biton expected to hear the television, but the apartment was strangely quiet. "Cavan?"

The door to Biton's room was open. Maybe he was asleep. A quick look showed the bed empty. Checking Erik's room, he found no sign of Cavan. Panic started a slow crawl through his stomach. Biton pushed back anxiety with rational thought. Cavan wouldn't have left the apartment, not when Biton told him not to. The front door was dead bolted when he came in. Only someone with a key could have locked it from the outside. Cavan had to be here.

"Cavan, come here." The stern tone usually exacted immediate obedience. Holding his breath, his ears strained to hear anything besides his beating heart. The sound of a door opening in his bedroom hurried him in that direction. "Cavan?"

Tear tracks still stained Cavan's face as he crawled out of the closet. "Master..." A gulping sob drew the word out.

Kneeling next to the distraught young man, Biton gathered him in his arms. "I'm here. It's okay." He didn't bother to ask why Cavan was hiding. Right now, the only thing that mattered was he was still here.

———

Biton rested his head on the back of the couch with his eyes closed. Snuggled into the crook of his arm, Cavan was quiet and his trembling had stopped. It took almost an hour to calm the terrified young man.

"Why were you hiding?" Pulling Cavan a little tighter, he nuzzled the soft red hair.

"I'm sorry."

"You didn't do anything wrong. I just want to know why. Was someone here?" The idea startled Biton. What would happen when Wainwright found out Cavan was pressing charges? The shiver of fear from the younger man made him keep that thought to himself.

"No..." Cavan ducked his face into Biton's chest. "I just... I never..." A deep breath preceded a spate of words. "My old master kept me locked in my cell when he wasn't home."

Biton rubbed the back of Cavan's neck. "What was your cell like?"

"Small. Blankets on the floor. A bucket for…you know."

"Were you always alone in there?" His hand moved down to rub Cavan's back in slow circles.

"Yes. Unless my master came to see me." His face still buried in Biton's chest muffled Cavan's words.

Biton's fingers caressed Cavan's chin and tugged his face up so he could see his eyes. "You won't stay in a cell here. This is your home, not your prison."

It would be so easy to mistake the gratitude lighting Cavan's eyes as something more. A slight move forward and their lips would meet. Biton ached to fall into his lips and take comfort in what Cavan innocently offered, but Dr. Merten's words held him back. Not knowing what to say, he pressed a chaste kiss on his brow. "We should get something to eat."

Disappointment replaced gratitude but Cavan just nodded.

Keeping his hands off would be hard, but Biton knew the doctor was right. Somehow, Cavan's well being replaced the desire that had drawn Biton out of his grief and back into the world.

Chapter Seven

"Come in," Biton said as he shook Antonio's hand. Nearly a week had passed since the interview with Ramos. Biton hadn't heard from either detective since then. "What brings you here?"

"Just wanted to update you on the case."

"Have they arrested Wainwright yet?" Biton led them into the living room.

"No."

Biton stopped short and turned. "Why the hell not?" Anger flared through him.

"Calm down. The prosecutor wants to build a bigger case against him."

"Bigger case? He tortured and sexually abused Cavan! How much bigger do you need?"

Antonio moved past Biton. "You know as well as I do, with his resources, arresting him on assault and battery, he'd be out on bail in a couple of hours.

Considering Cavan is a submissive, Wainwright's lawyers will argue their relationship was consensual. We can't charge him for child abuse in Cavan's case because the statute of limitations is only five years. And we have no proof of murder other than Cavan's assumption that Mateo didn't survive the beating."

Biton followed him into the living room and collapsed on the couch. Antonio was right. There wasn't much of a case and once they hauled Wainwright in for assault, any evidence available, including the slaves still under his control, could disappear.

"The DA thinks that if we can get more information on Mateo and what happened to him, we'll have a better chance of holding him without bail. Do you think Cavan could talk a little more coherently now?"

"Maybe. He knows you, trusts you more than he did Ramos. He only talked then because I told him he had to."

"How's he adapting to you?"

Biton wiped his hand down his face. "He's doing better. I had to leave him alone a few days ago and he hid in the closet while I was gone. Of course I haven't had to go anywhere since then. He's seeing a psychiatrist in a little while. Elizabeth Merten. Fortunately, she agreed to come here for the first few sessions. You should know her, or of her."

"Yeah, she's a bulldog for the prosecution. How much does she know?"

"Enough. I told Harry what was going on and I'm taking a leave of absence from the firm. If," he paused with a sigh, "When this hits the press, I want to minimize the damage to the firm."

"Cavan could come back and stay with us."

"No, my career can take the scrutiny. I have enough money to retire. Actually, I was thinking about it when you introduced me to Cavan."

"Because of grief; not because you wanted to."

Biton smiled at his friend. "You know me too well. And yes, Cavan has eased the constant tension I've felt since Erik died. But it's more than just a distraction."

Antonio laughed. "It's a good thing I don't bet with Lia. She would have won this one. She thought Cavan was perfect for you."

"I'm beginning to think she's right, but in the end, it'll be Cavan's choice. First he has to learn how the world works outside his cage. But we need to get Wainwright in his own cage and soon." Biton stood up. "I'll get him."

———

Cavan was happy to see Mr. Casala, but it didn't take long for the pleasure to fade. Thinking about Mateo made his memories of his own punishment too vivid.

"Cavan, I need to know what happened to Mateo after his beating. You said you thought he died. What made you think that?"

"He was barely breathing." Cavan kept his eyes down, his hands clasped tight together. "Master made us leave, go to our cells. I heard him swearing at Mateo, telling him he deserved to die for embarrassing him."

"Embarrassing him?"

"Some of the Master's friends were there. One of them wanted Mateo. I think the man was someone important. The Master acted different toward him."

"Different how?"

Cavan darted a quick look at Master Biton. "Like the man was his Master." Cavan sighed when Master Biton gave him an encouraging smile and a nod. "He even called him 'Sir'."

"Why did this man want Mateo?"

"Mateo was new. He'd only been there a few days. He couldn't even speak English." Cavan closed his eyes as he remembered the panicked chattering in the unknown language. "I don't think he was properly trained. He kept trying to stop the man from touching him. We had to tie him to the rack." His part in Mateo's fate still haunted him. The terrified man fought them hard. "By then, the Master's friend was so angry..." Cavan didn't want to talk about it any more. The memories flooding over him were too vivid, too real.

"Go on, Cavan, I have to know."

"There was so much blood, you know, after the man took him. He was so rough. He pulled Mateo's hair so hard, it came out in clumps. After the man finished, he told the Master he would have to do better next time. The Master was so mad... Mateo was still on the rack when he grabbed the whip." Taking a deep breath, he tried to push the memory away, but it wouldn't go. Tears spilled down his face.

Warmth embraced him when Master Biton's arms wrapped around him. Soft kisses covered his forehead. "What happened afterwards? Did you see Mateo again?"

Cavan leaned into his Master's embrace and shook his head. "No… But…"

"What Cavan?" His Master's voice was so gentle.

"I think we buried him…" He couldn't stop the sobs. "The next night, the Master made us carry a big box to a van… We had to ride with it. It smelled really bad. We drove a long time and then he made us dig a big hole and bury the box." Burying his face in Master Biton's neck, Cavan couldn't stop crying.

He'd never allowed himself to mourn for Mateo. Too afraid of finding the same fate, he forced the sadness into a small dark room in his mind, one reserved for all the pain and sorrow of his life. With the door to the room forced open, all the terror, all the pain flooded into the daylight.

———

Biton held the shaking young man close as sobs poured out of him. It was as if a floodgate opened and all the sorrow of his life came out at once. "Cavan, it's okay. It's over. You don't have to endure that ever again." His words did nothing to staunch the flow.

Hysterical words fell from Cavan's lips too garbled to understand.

"Please, Cavan. You'll make yourself sick." He rubbed the tense back with strong strokes. "You're safe.

I won't let anything happen to you. I promise."

Still the tears flowed. Biton rained kisses over his hair, crooning comforting words, but to no avail. Hysteria had a strong hold on the terrified young man.

"Antonio, my cell phone, it's on the table. Call Dr. Merten. She should be here soon but…"

Antonio had watched the scene with a helpless expression. He jumped up at the chance to do something.

Out of the corner of his eye, Biton saw Antonio grab the phone and scrolled through the phone list.

"Calm down, Cavan." Using a stronger tone, he hoped the years of training would make his sobbing lover obey. Still grief racked the slender body. More grief than could be explained by the death of Mateo. Biton understood what was happening but he felt lost, not knowing how to comfort Cavan, not wanting to see him in so much pain.

His need to dominate someone, to inflict exquisite pain on a helpless but willing body, didn't include emotional pain. Erik had been happy with him, with their life together. Although he died far too young, Erik insisted he wouldn't have wanted his life any other way. Biton had made him happy and he took comfort in that knowledge when Erik died.

Cavan had never known happiness at any level. Pain was just pain and sorrow ruled his existence. As Biton held his distraught lover close, the decision to give up whatever part of his life Cavan couldn't handle seemed easy. He would use all his resources to ensure

Cavan's happiness rivaled Erik's.

The cell phone snapping shut brought his attention back to Antonio. "What did she say?"

"She's about five minutes away and she has sedatives in her bag. She said to keep trying to calm him until she gets here." Antonio knelt near the couch, his hand reached out to rub Cavan's shoulder. "We won't let anyone hurt you again, Cavan. And I'll make sure Wainwright pays for what he did to you and Mateo and all the others. That's what the police do, Cavan. That's why I had to ask you all those questions."

Biton managed a small grim smile at his friend. Nothing helped to calm Cavan. He only hoped the doctor arrived soon.

———

Dopey from the shot of strong sedative, Cavan's body was almost limp against Biton.

The doctor's dark eyes took in the scene with a slight frown. "What brought it on?"

"I was questioning him. I'm Detective Antonio Casala." He offered his hand to the doctor.

She shook it almost as an afterthought. "You probably shouldn't try to get information until he's had some therapy first."

"Can't wait. It appears Wainwright's added murder to assault and battery charges. I need to know what happened and Cavan's the only witness."

"I understand, but do you really think you'll get anything out of him if the memory causes this type

111

of reaction?" She waved her hand in Cavan's general direction.

"I think it was more than the memory of one incident." Biton still rocked his now calm lover. "I couldn't make out much of what he was saying but I think it was everything, his life until now."

"Maybe he's realized it's over." Dr. Merten's severe look gentled. "That would be helpful in his recovery. Sometimes it takes years to get to that point."

"I hope he knows it's over." Biton continued to cuddle the half-asleep man to his chest. After dropping a gentle kiss against the now relaxed brow, he glanced up at his guests. "I won't let him be hurt anymore."

Dr. Merten's lips quirked a slight smile. "I believe you, but does he?"

"I think so." He looked down at the peaceful face. "I hope so. He comes to me when he's scared. I take that as a sign he knows I'll protect him."

"Dr. Merten, do you think he'll be able to answer some more questions?" Antonio asked.

"Probably not today. I gave him a pretty strong dose."

"He said Wainwright made them bury the body of another slave. I have to know where. If I can link a body to Wainwright, he'll go away forever. I need information."

"It didn't sound like he'd be able to help you locate it, Antonio." Biton wanted Wainwright locked up, but he wasn't sure he could handle watching Cavan suffer through questioning again. Not if it upset him like it had today.

"Not today," Dr. Merten said. "Maybe tomorrow, but I want to be here. I can give him a mild sedative to help keep him calm before you start."

"Thank you," Biton said before his gaze drifted back to Cavan.

In his sleep, Cavan's lips moved. His fingers, still curled around Biton's arm, tightened.

Biton sent a silent prayer that his dreams were peaceful. Ignoring the inquisitive eyes of the good doctor, Biton brushed a kiss against Cavan's lips.

———

Cavan hadn't stirred when Antonio helped Biton get him into bed. Dr. Merten checked his vitals before she left. She said he'd probably sleep through the night and she was right.

Biton held him close in the early morning light. A couple of times he woke to hear Cavan's mumbled dreams but he settled as soon as Biton touched him. The strength of Cavan's trust in him comforted Biton Only a week had passed since Cavan came to his house for a simple lunch. As many times as Biton wondered what he'd gotten himself into, he'd also thanked fate for bringing Cavan into his life.

The deep abiding grief over Erik wasn't gone, never would be completely, but Cavan had chased away the worst of the pain. It only seemed fair for Biton to exorcize Cavan's demons. Only three weeks remained on their temporary agreement. If things had been different, he would have already permanently claimed Cavan as his. But it wasn't his decision alone and Cavan wasn't able to make an objective choice.

As Cavan stirred against him, Biton moved away. The last few days, he managed to avoid sex by telling Cavan he was tired. Unfortunately, his body wouldn't go along with the charade. His swollen erection gave truth to his lies. He wanted Cavan so bad it hurt, but the doctor was right and he knew it the minute she said it. Sex would muddy up Cavan's recovery so instead of enjoying the slender body, Biton made do with cold showers and secretive hand jobs.

"Good morning," he whispered as Cavan's eyes opened.

His eyelashes blinked several times before Cavan turned his head to look at Biton. "Master?"

"I'm here." Biton ran a hand through the soft red hair. The idea of Cavan's short hair shoulder length ran through his mind. He wanted to tell him to grow it out but then stopped. That was another decision Cavan should learn to make. He smiled at the younger man. The humorous idea that Cavan's retraining had become his own made his smile widen. "How are you feeling?"

"Achy…" Cavan turned his head from side to side, stretching his neck muscles. "What happened?"

"You don't remember?"

"Mr. Casala was here…" Cavan rubbed his eyes and sat up. A frown creased his brow. "He asked me some questions."

"Yes, and it upset you."

Nodding, Cavan closed his eyes. "Master?"

"Yes?"

"Am I in trouble now? For helping..." A soft sob choked his words.

"Shhh..." Biton sat up next to him and slipped his arm around him. "No, never in trouble for telling the truth."

"But I helped the Master. I helped him bu..."

"You had no choice. Don't think about it now. Antonio will be here later with Dr. Merten. Until then, you don't have to worry."

Cavan leaned into him, his arms wrapped around Biton. The warm lean body pressed against him made it difficult to resist temptation.

Biton pulled away from him before his willpower deserted him. "You need to eat something. Go get a shower and I'll fix us some food" Rolling out of bed, he grabbed his robe, hoping it would hide his arousal.

"Master?" An obvious bulge tenting the sheet at Cavan's groin explained the wistful tone in his voice.

He leaned over and kissed Cavan's forehead. "Go. Shower." Biton hurried from the room before he decided the doctor was full of it.

"Hi Cavan, we really didn't get to meet yesterday. You were a little upset when I got here." Dr. Merten's sweet smile didn't seem to reassure Cavan and he looked confused when she held out her hand. She pulled it back after a few awkward seconds.

Biton stood back watching. As far as he could tell, except for Lia, it had been years since Cavan had anything to do with a woman. He chose Dr. Merten based on her credentials, but maybe he should have considered her gender as well. "Cavan, this is the doctor I told you about."

Cavan hadn't been happy about talking to yet another person and proof of his discomfort showed on his face now. Biton considered his expression a good sign. Normally, a submissive wouldn't show any displeasure at his Master's request.

Dr. Merten acted as if there was nothing unusual about his behavior. "Cavan, yesterday talking to Detective Casala upset you so much, I had to give you some medicine to calm down. Today, he wants to ask you some more questions but this time, I'm going to give you the medicine first. It will help keep you calm."

Cavan's eyes darted toward Antonio before he met Biton's gaze.

Nodding his approval at the bewildered young man, he smiled. "It's okay, Cavan. We should do what she says."

Dr. Merten nodded and opened the small black bag she brought with her. "This will just be a little pin prick, Cavan, and then you'll start to feel a little sleepy. Okay?" She turned a little bottle upside down and stuck a hypodermic through the rubber seal.

Biton glanced at Cavan's pale face.

His eyes followed the doctor's every move.

"Cavan, it's okay. I promise."

Cavan jumped slightly at Biton's voice and turned to look at him. His hand lifted toward Biton then fell.

"Oh, the hell with it," Biton mumbled. Sitting next to Cavan, he wrapped his arm around the nervous man's shoulders.

Tension shed off him like water sheeting off a roof as Cavan relaxed into Biton's embrace. His head tilted toward Biton's shoulder as he exhaled a long sigh of relief.

Biton silently dared the doctor to say anything, but her arched eyebrow lowered when she looked at Cavan.

A quick nod was her only comment. "Roll up your sleeve, Cavan." When he complied, she injected him quickly.

Biton shared the slight flinch of his reaction, but other than that, Cavan didn't move from his embrace.

"It should take effect quickly." She busied herself packing up her implements as Antonio pulled a chair over near Cavan.

"How are you feeling, Cavan?" Antonio's voice was gentle and low.

"A little dizzy…sir."

"That's the medicine taking effect, Cavan. It's normal." Dr. Merten sat in the other chair across from the couch. "Tell me if you feel nauseous."

Cavan nodded but didn't look at the woman.

"Yesterday, you said Wainwright took you in a van somewhere to bury a box." Antonio kept his voice low, soothing.

"Yes, sir," Cavan mumbled.

"Do you remember when this was?"

"At night…"

"I mean, was it this year, last year?"

"I don't know. The days all seem the same."

Antonio frowned.

Biton could almost see his thoughts. How would Cavan know when? He wasn't allowed to watch television or read a newspaper. Years of his life passed without a way to count the days.

"Was it winter? Cold out when you were digging or was it hot, like summer?"

"Winter. There were lots of pretty lights on the windows of houses." Cavan's words slurred a little.

"Like Christmas lights? Do you remember Christmas?"

"Yeah… From a long time ago." Cavan nodded and looked at Biton. A small smile quirked his lips. "I remember Christmas."

"So was it Christmas lights?" Antonio asked again.

"Yeah… Yes, sir." Cavan's head bobbed as the drugs took full effect.

Biton glanced at Dr. Merten, but she didn't seem concerned.

"Was it around the time you were hospitalized?"

"Yes, sir… He… I kept thinking… I didn't want to be the next box…" His voice cracked slightly.

Biton could feel the tension returning to Cavan's shoulders. "It's okay, babe." He kissed Cavan's temple. "You're doing good."

Antonio shifted his gaze to Biton. "Last Christmas.

Four months ago." Returning his attention to Cavan, Antonio asked, "Did you see where the van went? Anything that might help us find the box? Like a street sign or a city sign?"

"I don't remember…"

Dr. Merten leaned forward. "Cavan, do you not remember or you don't want to?"

"I'm not supposed to tell… I've said too much." Cavan turned to Biton. "Please, Master, he'll kill me too…"

Caressing Cavan's cheek, Biton leaned in to brush his lips with a kiss. "No he won't, Cavan. If we find that box, Wainwright will go to prison and he'll never get out. You, and others like you, will be safe. You don't want anyone else to suffer like you and Mateo. We have to find the box."

His eyes filling with tears, Cavan nodded. He turned his head to kiss Biton's palm before he looked up at Antonio again. "It was a funny name. I don't know how to say it but it started with 'mama'."

"Mamaroneck?" Antonio looked at Biton. "Wainwright has a home in Mamaroneck. Would he dare bury the evidence on his own property?"

"Why not? He has no idea anyone would think to look there." Biton hugged Cavan a little tighter. Except Cavan knew. He vowed not to let Cavan out of his sight until Wainwright was safely behind bars. "Cavan's statement should be enough for a search warrant."

Antonio nodded as he stood up. "You've done very well, Cavan. Very well. Thank you. Biton, I'll let you know what's going on." He walked toward the doorway with the speed of a man on a mission. Almost as an afterthought, he turned back to Dr. Merten. "Doctor, thank you, too. I hope you can help Cavan. He's a good kid. He deserves some happiness."

Biton couldn't agree more.

───

Unwilling to disturb the half-asleep man in his arms, Biton let the doctor find her way out. Tension from the interview crept out of him as he nuzzled Cavan's hair. If they found the body, Wainwright's money wouldn't help him. Once the details of the case were presented, Biton was sure the man would be held without bail.

Monday, Cavan would start therapy with Dr. Merten. Until he felt comfortable with the woman, they would meet here, with Biton close by. How long the therapy would last was unknown. More than the twenty-one days left on the contract, that much was certain.

───

Biton stood in the doorway of the bedroom watching Cavan sleep. The first session with Dr. Merten took a lot out of both of them. In the end, she sedated Cavan again. Biton wanted to go to him and hold him while he slept, but the temptation of the warm lean body against his would be too much. Instead of tucking Cavan into his own bed, he put him in Erik's room. He couldn't sleep next to him anymore or Dr. Merten's advice would be history. As much as he hated not being able to make love to Cavan, it was best if he controlled his desires.

The trill of his phone pulled him out of his thoughts. Closing the door, he hurried to catch the phone before the noise woke Cavan. "Savakis."

"Biton, it's Antonio. We have him."

"Wainwright?"

"Yes. The body is in the morgue and Wainwright is in custody. He's screaming his head off about false arrest, but he's not going anywhere. Arraignment will be in the morning."

"Do you have enough to deny bail?"

"I think so. But you never know until it happens."

"Does he know it was Cavan who informed?" Biton paced the length of the living room. The last thing he wanted was for Wainwright to know about Cavan.

"He wasn't told, but I think I heard him mumble his name when we were bringing him in."

Biton closed his eyes and forced his breathing to some normalcy. "What about his house? Other victims?"

"I have the warrant already and I'm on my way there now."

A sigh of relief forced its way out of Biton's lungs. "Good. That's good. Keep me posted." He shut the phone off as he dropped to the couch. Cavan was safe now.

"Master?"

Biton jerked around to see Cavan standing in the doorway. "Hey, you should be asleep."

"I had a… You weren't there…" He ducked his head, but the worried lip biting was still visible.

"Come here." Biton motioned for him to join him on the couch.

Cavan didn't hesitate. A soft sigh teased Biton's neck as Cavan curled up under his arm.

"Bad dream?"

A nod was the only answer.

"Time for your nightmares to end." Biton smiled down at the curious green eyes. "Antonio called. Wainwright is in jail and he's not likely to get out again. Your life is yours now, Cavan, to do whatever you want to do."

"I want to stay with you." The green eyes were so open, so innocent and, God help him, so sincere.

"Cavan, you can't know what you want. You've never known anything except abuse. Being submissive is more than accepting pain or obeying orders."

"You don't hurt me. You make me feel good." A small frown creased his forehead.

Biton smiled and shook his head. "But I've wanted to do things to you…things you might not understand. I want to be rough, to see you helpless and bound and begging…"

Fear flitted through Cavan's eyes, but he didn't look away.

"But the whole time I'm doing things to you, I want you to feel pleasure in it not pain for pain's sake, not pain for my sake. I want you to feel it because you want it and you want me. Until I'm sure it's your choice, I won't do it. I won't touch you."

"Is that why you put me in the other room?"

Biton sighed and let his hand caress Cavan's cheek. "Yes. And that's why you have to stay in the other room."

"You don't want me anymore? You want Erik?"

Biton couldn't stop the tears in his eyes. "Yes, I want Erik. How did you know about him?"

"You sometimes whisper his name in your sleep."

Biton swallowed past the lump in his throat. "We were together for ten years. I loved him very much."

Cavan's fingers captured the escaping tears. "Why don't you get him back?"

A small sob caught in Biton's throat. "If there was a way to get him back I would. But he died, Cavan. He got sick and died."

For the first time, Cavan's arms wrapped around Biton without prompting. "I'm sorry, Master. I didn't know."

"I didn't think to tell you." He hugged Cavan tight against him. "Our 'get to know each other' lunch turned out a little different than I expected."

"Did you do all those things…the things you want to do to me…did you do them with Erik?"

"Yes, but Erik knew his limits. He'd tell me if it was too much or not enough. He enjoyed our games as much as I did."

"I could do it. Do what you want."

123

Biton sniffed and ran the back of his hand across his eyes. "I know you could, but I don't know if you'd tell me when to stop. That is the most important part of being dominant or submissive, knowing the limits."

"I could do that..." The quiver in Cavan's voice betrayed his fear.

"Maybe someday, but not now." Biton kissed his hair. "Now we concentrate on making you better." He hugged him a little tighter. "And to do that, you have to start sleeping in the other bedroom."

"That's why you haven't...you know..."

"Yes," Biton sighed. "That's why we haven't 'you know'd'." A final kiss to Cavan's brow. "Come on. We should start something for dinner."

Chapter Eight

Even after three weeks of sleeping alone, Cavan still missed the warmth of his Master's body against him. Well, not really slept. Tossed, turned and woke with nightmares. After spending years sleeping alone on a cold floor, he should be able to sleep in a comfortable warm bed. When he slept with his Master, he didn't have restless nights.

His old Master was in jail now. Three other slaves had been found at his home, one of them very young, according to Mr. Casala. His old Master would stay in jail until the trial. That part of his life was over, except for testifying against Master...

No, not Master, the man's name was Wainwright. Dr. Merten said he had to stop thinking of anyone as his master or himself as a slave. But he wanted to be a slave to Master Biton. To Biton... Although, he had permission to use his name, Cavan couldn't bring himself to do it even in his thoughts.

The contract would be over in a couple of days. Each sleepless night meant one more day was gone. Time never meant anything to him before. His old life was endless pain and humiliation. Between his cell and his time in the Master's dungeon, there was nothing to mark the days.

His time spent with Master Biton seemed too short, flashing by as fast as a blink of an eye. He was learning things, which according to Master Biton, he would need to live his own life. He enjoyed their sessions together. His Master worked with him daily on stuff he vaguely remembered from school. Reading was something he'd come to love. Math still gave him fits.

Even the short trips shopping weren't as scary as he thought they'd be, especially when they went to the bookstore. He loved the smell of all the books mixed with the rich aroma of coffee. Clothes shopping wasn't as much fun, but it seemed to please his Master to buy him things.

They had even gone out to eat several times. Cavan grinned at the memory of the sushi he'd tried. He didn't like it, but was afraid his Master would be mad it he said so. But Master Biton kept insisting truthfulness was necessary. He had swallowed his fear with the raw fish and told him he didn't like it. His Master just laughed and ordered him something that was cooked.

He still found it hard to call his Master by his name, but he'd managed to stop calling him Master when they were in public. Small steps, the Master said.

Small steps forward were better than standing still.

The hardest part was talking to Dr. Merten. She seemed nice enough, but Cavan wanted to forget his past, not relive it.

Cavan sighed as he rolled over. The things Wainwright did to him were cruel and wrong. He understood that now. It still terrified him even though his former master was in jail and would be there for a very long time.

But Biton never really hurt him. Even the first time, when he strapped him into the sling, Cavan hadn't been afraid. The ache of arousal had blanked out all the bad memories of being bound and helpless.

The thought worked its way through his mind. Why had it been so different? The reason struck him almost as hard as a blow. He trusted Biton. And it made all the difference in the world.

Only a couple of days left on the contract... Cavan rolled over again and stared at the dim light of the sunrise shining through the window. The contract said Cavan had to obey Master Biton. And if he didn't... Cavan's lips curled into a slight smile as a plan formed.

———

Biton frowned as he walked into the living room. It took most of the night for him to finally fall asleep and to wake early to a blaring TV wasn't something he expected or desired. He found Cavan dressed in a robe and stretched out on the couch. The TV screen flipped rapidly from one channel to the next. Evidently, Cavan had paid attention when Biton showed him how to use it.

"Cavan! What are you doing?"

"Couldn't sleep." The half-mumbled tone was almost inaudible over the jumbled sound from the television.

"Turn that thing down." Biton's head hurt enough from lack of sleep and endless thoughts about Cavan leaving him without the additional noise.

"I like it loud…"

Biton could almost feel his eyebrows touch his hairline. "You what?" The growl didn't get a response from Cavan. Or did it?

Did his chest rise a little more rapidly? Was that a tremble in the hand holding the remote? "I said I like it loud." The words were a little more forceful, almost defiant.

Shaking sleep from his mind, Biton realized Cavan hadn't called him Master or Sir even once. He marched over to the couch and snatched the remote from Cavan's hand. After turning the TV off, he tossed the remote on the side table. "What game are you playing, Cavan?"

A little fear crept into the pale green eyes. "The contract… You said we had to follow the contract."

Biton bit his lip to keep a smile from forming.

"If I'm bad, you have to punish me…" His voice trailed off.

"And do you think you need to be punished?"

Cavan nodded slowly as the fear faded from his

eyes. Lip biting became the norm as Cavan mimicked Biton's attempt to stop a grin.

Heat pooled in Biton's groin. The restraint of the last three weeks freed, he was hard in seconds. "Stand up." The growl garnered immediate compliance.

Cavan's tented robe confirmed his real interest in the expected punishment. His smile faded and only longing colored his eyes now. A furtive tongue quickly wet his lips.

Biton resisted kissing him. He was to be punished, not rewarded. "Follow me." He turned and walked toward the playroom without looking to see if Cavan obeyed. The soft pad of bare feet followed him.

The scent of leather washed over him as he opened the door. The ache in his groin intensified when he flipped on the dim overhead lights. For obvious reasons, the windows were covered in this room, but Biton preferred soft lighting reminiscent of dawn or dusk.

Glancing around the room, his mind had trouble choosing a course of action. Even if Cavan pushed him to do something, Biton didn't want to go too far. His slave was still fragile from his previous life.

He glanced at the soft leather sling. Being so close made it tempting, but he pushed the thought aside. He wanted full access to Cavan.

His eyes flitted around the room before resting on the iron pillory. Secured between two floor-to-ceiling posts, it exposed both the front and back of the slave. With restraints for the head and wrists, the upright version of stocks would be perfect. Unlike stocks, the pillory's design allowed the submissive's head and neck to remain straight instead of forcing the neck to remain bent forward. The ankle restraints would hold his legs spread allowing Biton to tease and torment as well as take him.

He tugged at his aching balls. A cock ring would help suppress his immediate desires. Maybe one for Cavan as well.

Biton schooled his expression back to stern before he turned around. "Strip," he barked.

The harsh tone caused a startled jump from Cavan, but he shed the robe as if it burned him. His cock jutted out proud, already weeping. His pale flesh trembled and his breathing quickened.

Temptation flowed over Biton to drop to his knees and suck Cavan off right there. But so much more than simple gratification was at stake here. Dr. Merten's words whispered to him, but he pushed them aside. Cavan's deliberate disobedience was a good sign in Biton's mind. If Cavan could enjoy small sessions… Biton realized how much he wanted to keep Cavan, but at the same time how much he needed to release his dominant side. If both were possible, even in small measure…

"Over there." Biton pointed to the pillory.

A slight frown creased Cavan's forehead, but he didn't hesitate. He stepped into position, his legs apart and feet planted close to the ankle shackles. His gaze glued to the floor, he rested his neck on the metal collar.

Sweet arousal swept through Biton at the sight of Cavan's submission. With trembling fingers, he adjusted the top rack for Cavan's height. He latched the neck and wrist restraints on the horizontal bar. Kneeling to lock Cavan's legs apart, being face level with the dripping cock was too much temptation to pass up. He ran his tongue around the tip gathering the bitter moisture before sucking gently. Moans from above rewarded his actions. He pulled away before he pushed Cavan over the edge to release. Facing his willing captive, he let the feeling of power merge with intense sexual desire. He had missed this part of his life more than he realized.

Leaning close, he brushed his lips against Cavan's then whispered, "Listen to me carefully, Cavan. I told you part of the game is knowing your limits and letting me know them as well. Do you understand what I'm saying?"

Cavan nodded as much as the restraint would allow.

"If things get to be too much, you have to tell me. Sometimes saying 'stop' just isn't enough. So we need safe words." Biton ran his hand down Cavan's chest and stomach. He paused just before the hard erection.

"Safe…words, Master?"

"Yes, safe words let me know you are okay or my actions are too much." His hand made the final move to Cavan's cock.

A sharp gasp accompanied a long slow stroke. "Master…please…"

Biton's pleasure spiked at the plea. He nuzzled

Cavan's hair as he smiled. "So if you say 'red', I'll stop. 'Yellow', I'll ease off or slow down and 'green', means more or go ahead. Do you understand?" His question accompanied another strong pull of Cavan's hard flesh.

"Yes…Master…green…please…"

Biton chuckled. His slave was so close to coming. And so was Biton.

"I'll be right back." With a soft kiss and quick tease of his hand along the heated erection, Biton moved across the room.

At the tall chest of drawers, he paused to clear his head and shed his robe. All the things he wanted to do to Cavan cluttered his mind. "Keep it simple," he mumbled as he opened the top drawer.

A pair of nipple clamps, a couple of leather cock rings… Dropping the clamps and one cock ring on the top of the dresser, he paused to wrap the other leather ring around his cock and balls. Pulling it tight, he fastened it with the Velcro closure. He closed the first drawer and opened another. A cock flogger found its way to the small pile accumulating on the dresser. A couple of condoms, lube…

Glancing back at Cavan first, he walked over to the wall racks. Whips and paddles hung in a neat row. Biton fingered a leather flogger but decided against it. The memory of Wainwright's brutal whipping still gave Cavan nightmares. The wide selection of whips would probably need to be removed. Settling on a lightweight wooden paddle, he gathered up his other toys and started back toward his immobilized lover.

A fleeting thought made him turn back to the toy chest. Opening yet another drawer, he picked out a medium sized butt plug. When the time came, Biton wanted him open and ready.

Either from fear or inattention, Cavan's erection drooped at half-mast.

Biton placed his toys, except the cock ring, on a small table near the pillory. "Do you want to stop?"

Cavan shook his head slightly.

"What do you say?"

"Green, Master, green."

Biton rewarded him with a quick pinch to his nipples. "Good."

The wilting flesh bobbed with interest.

Sliding the cock ring under Cavan's balls, Biton tightened and fastened it with practiced hands. "Today, you can't cum until I tell you. Understand?"

"Yes Master."

"But when you do…" Biton inhaled deep as a shiver of desire swept over him. His mouth close to Cavan's ear, he whispered, "When you do, it'll be so good."

The shiver transferred to Cavan and his cock rose to full attention.

Walking slowly around his captive, Biton trailed his fingers across sensitive flesh. Coming to a stop behind Cavan, he dipped one finger into the crack of his ass, running it down teasing the pale flesh. A soft muffled moan made him smile.

A stinging slap to one of the sweet round globes

caused a sharp gasp. A second glancing blow to the other cheek drew a moaned exhale.

Moving around the bound man, Biton snagged the nipple clamps from the table. Tugging the chain to test its strength, he finally came to rest facing his captive. Cavan's hard weeping cock reassured Biton. His fingers teased the already hardened nipples. "Still okay?"

"Yes..." Cavan's eyes rolled as Biton's fingers tightened on his flesh. "Master..."

Leaning over to suck hard on a tiny nipple, Biton's fingers pinched the other. When his teeth grazed the tender flesh, Cavan's body jerked but the moan wasn't one of pain.

After releasing the hard wet nipple, Biton slipped on a clamp, letting it tighten slowly.

"Master!"

"Too much?"

"Green!" The hard flesh straining up toward Biton confirmed Cavan's emphatic response.

Licking a line across Cavan's chest, he treated the other nipple with the same care. With both nipples bound, Biton tugged gently at the chain connecting them.

"Yes, Master..." Cavan's body arched toward Biton as far as the pillory would allow. His cock brushed Biton's.

Biton grabbed his balls and yanked to keep from coming. As much as he wanted this to last, he wasn't sure even a cock ring would slow his climax. The idea of burying himself in Cavan's sweet tight ass was almost too much. He turned away from the luscious sight of pale helpless flesh to regain control.

"Master?" Concern and desire tinged the word.

Biton shook his head. "It's... I just need a second." Control was Biton's world but at the moment, he wasn't doing a very good job at it. Turning back to his bound lover, he smiled his reassurance. "I'm okay." With a sharp tug on the chain, he leaned forward and captured Cavan's lips with his. He nipped at the thin lips until they opened.

Cavan accepted his tongue with a relieved sigh and an enthusiastic response. Tongues tangled as Cavan's neck strained against his restraints. A soft whimper curled in his throat when their lips parted. "Master..."

"What do you want, Cavan?" Biton ran his hands down his slave's sides and around to grasp his ass. "Tell me how you feel."

"Want you... Feel you..." Cavan gasped as inquisitive fingers parted his cheeks and slid down the warm crevice. "Yes... Green, Master..."

Biton smiled at his response.

The safe word seemed to be Cavan's only way to express what he wanted. It would do for now.

He pushed one finger against the tiny puckered hole.

Cavan's body strained against its bonds as he pushed into the finger.

Biton pulled away and released his hold on the younger man. Walking around to the small table, he grabbed the lube. With a generous portion squeezed into his palm, he picked up the butt plug. As he smeared the lube on the rubber toy, he moved behind Cavan. With a slick finger, he pushed between the firm ass cheeks and plunged into Cavan's hole with no warning.

"Oh… yeah…" Cavan's body shook at the invasion, but his tone wasn't of pain. He rolled his ass against Biton's hand, working the finger deeper.

A second finger joined the first. Biton leaned close to Cavan's ear. "Don't cum. Remember, you can't cum until I tell you to." His fingers bent to stroke the hard knot of Cavan's prostate. "Don't cum!"

Cavan cried out as pleasure shook his body.

Biton reached around with his free hand to find the hard cock weeping with an almost constant flow of pre-come, but he had obeyed. Twisting his fingers around and spreading them, he opened the tight hole farther. Slipping free of the velvet heat, he then pressed the tip of the cone shaped butt plug against the opening. Slow, steady pressure and the plug slid home. He pushed the protruding end down slightly, forcing the hard rubber up against Cavan's prostate.

"Yellow!" The bound body shuddered hard and convulsed.

Cavan's shout startled him and he released his hold on the plug. Wrapping his arms around the tense body, he kissed his neck. "What's wrong? Did I hurt you? Do I need to stop?"

Cavan's chest rose and fell swiftly under Biton's hands. "I was… I… I didn't… Couldn't stop! I'm sorry, Master…" The shudder turned to shaking as Cavan's voice choked with sobs.

Biton grinned as his hands slid down to Cavan's cock.

Sure enough, Cavan had disobeyed. Slick seed dripped from his still hard cock.

"You've been bad, haven't you?"

"Yes, Master…" Sobs caught his breath and shook him.

Biton gathered the pungent liquid with his fingers, smearing it up Cavan's chest. With two fingers pressed against Cavan's lips, he whispered, "Taste yourself…"

In spite of the ragged breath, Cavan's mouth opened. Slow sucking pressure surrounded Biton's fingers. With Cavan's back tight against him, Biton rolled his hips, his cock sliding in the lube slick crack of the firm ass. The knot of the plug caught against his tight aching balls. "I think you deserve a spanking for disobeying me."

A soft moan vibrated around Biton's fingers. Biting his lips against the urge to replace the plug with his cock, he pulled his fingers free of the wet sucking heat. He backed away from temptation. Walking around in front of Cavan, he looked at his slave closely. His breathing was rapid but his eyes held no real fear. The straining cock hadn't lost any of its hardness in spite of the cum strewn across the floor and parts of Cavan's body. Bending over, Biton took the wet dick into his mouth and savored the bitter taste of come.

Cavan's hips jerked as if he didn't know whether to thrust into the pleasure or pull away.

His moans were sweet music to Biton, but he released him and straightened up. Close enough for their cocks to touch, Biton softly growled in Cavan's ear, "You have to be punished for the mess you've made."

He turned and strode back to the table. The light wooden paddle was one of his favorites. The weight made for very fine control and the delicately etched grooves always left an interesting pattern on a well-spanked ass. He clenched his hand around the handle to find the perfect balance. Standing beside Cavan, he waited. Anticipation was half the fun of a good spanking. For his part, he savored the moment before the wood made contact, almost a meditation. As for his slave, well, catching him off guard when the first blow landed thrilled Biton in ways he couldn't describe.

A sudden idea struck him. Laying the paddle on the table, he hurried across the room to the toy chest then opened a drawer. His eyes and hands searched quickly. With his prize clutched in his hands, he hurried back to Cavan.

With practiced, although shaking hands, Biton wrapped soft black silk several times around Cavan's head, blinding him. "Are you okay?" he asked the trembling man.

"Yes Master…"

"Good… Very good." Now, when Biton struck the first blow, Cavan wouldn't know until the paddle hit him.

The paddle retrieved, Biton rolled the handle

between his palms as he paced around his captive. Clenching the paddle in one hand with a firm grasp, he reached with the other and tugged at the chain dangling between the nipple clamps. A soft moan from parted lips encouraged him to yank a little harder.

As he moved around the bound body, he let his fingers trail around Cavan's waist until the post holding the pillory forced him to lift his hand. Thoughts of suspending Cavan from the ceiling hook next time ran through his mind.

Once again facing the enticing ass, Biton flexed his wrist, testing the balance of the paddle. With his other hand, he stroked Cavan's back. Stepping back, he positioned himself for the first blow. His cock leaked almost constantly with anticipation. He wondered if he could cum from just striking Cavan. Not that he wanted to. That pleasure was for Cavan's tight hot hole. A quick yank to his balls helped settle the urge for now. But he wouldn't be able to wait much longer. The pain of over-stimulation was almost too much to handle.

With a quick swing, wood met flesh. The satisfying jolt of the blow sent pleasure through Biton's arm and straight to his aching cock.

Cavan jumped, a cry forced from his body with a rush of air.

Biton admired the pale flesh turning red with a crisscross pattern of white. Raising the paddle again, he struck the other cheek. Again, a blush of rose colored Cavan's ass. A third strike muddied the white lines with red. A fourth followed quickly as he alternated sides.

Sweat trickled down Cavan's back, pooling in the dip where his round ass started. The muscles in his neck and back stood out as he prepared for the next blow.

Rolling the handle of the paddle between his palms, Biton waited for the tension to ease. He wanted to keep him off guard, not knowing when the next strike would come, but the taut flesh refused to relax.

Moving back to the table, he set the paddle down and picked up the cock flogger. With silent steps, he walked around to face his unseeing captive. Threading his fingers through the soft leather strands, he admired the view.

The short red hair plastered against his head and the blindfold damp with sweat from Cavan's forehead. His thin lips were caught between anxious teeth. His arms strained against the wrist shackles, forcing the lean muscles to bulge. Wet trails of sweat colored his chest. Jutted out hard and proud, his cock looked as if he hadn't already cum once.

Biton briefly envied him his youth.

This is what gave Biton the most pleasure. Helpless, bound, and still wanting, a willing slave gave Biton what he needed from a relationship. Was it wrong? What was done to Cavan before was. There was no doubt in his mind about that. But this…

"Green, Master…" Cavan panted as his body trembled. "Green… Please…"

"Say you want more. Don't hide behind the word 'green'. Tell me you want more…"

His body jumped as Biton's voice gave away his

change in position but his words didn't falter. "More, Master... More... Yes, please... I want more..."

Biton ran the soft leather strands of the cock flogger over Cavan's angry red erection.

"More..." was the strangled response.

A gentle swat of the flogger across Cavan's cock didn't stop the frantic pleas. Again, harder, Biton swung the small whip and his willing slave begged for yet more.

With hurried steps, Biton returned to the table, tossing the flogger aside for the paddle. He didn't pause until he was in position again behind Cavan. A harder blow than the others marked a round cheek.

"Yes, Master... Take me... I'm yours... I want to be yours..."

Another blow, and another, and Cavan's cries rambled into begging for more and wanting Biton.

And it was too much. Biton needed relief. The pain of the cock ring and the need for release made him dizzy with desire. Dropping the paddle to the floor, he stepped close to Cavan. With one hand, he pulled the butt plug free, while the other ripped open the Velcro closure on his cock ring. Both fell to the floor near the paddle.

Then, with one hard stroke, his aching cock was balls deep in sweet velvet heat. Hanging on to the top of the pillory, he pulled back and thrust hard, and again. Holding steady with one hand, the other reached around and yanked the cock ring from Cavan's dick. One arm tight around Cavan's chest, he wrapped the other around his waist and pulled at Cavan's hot swollen flesh. He growled in Cavan's ear, "Cum with me, Cavan. Now!"

The tight hole contracted around him as his slave obeyed. Biton's seed raced for freedom adding scalding heat to the already molten passage. "Oh, God, yes!" His cries matched Cavan's as exquisite release shook his body.

"Biton…"

The sound of Cavan shouting his name shook him. "You called my name…" In four weeks of living with him, Cavan hadn't been able to use his name without the title of Master.

"Please don't make me leave, Biton. I love you. I don't want to leave." Sobs racked Cavan's body where pleasure had so recently gripped him.

Biton's throat caught with emotion. "You don't have to…" he whispered. "You never have to."

"The contract… Tomorrow…"

"We'll draw up another." Biton squeezed the shaking man with one arm while his other reached for the release on the pillory. Cavan's freed torso sank into Biton's chest. He lowered him carefully to the floor, his legs still trapped by the bottom of the device.

Biton left him sprawled on the floor while he moved around to undo his legs. Pulling him up, Biton held him close. "You don't have to leave."

Cavan's face buried in his neck, his words were muffled. "Another thirty days?"

"No, we'll make this one longer."

The shaking eased and the sobs dropped to sniffling. "Longer?"

"Yeah, how does forever sound?" Biton's hands caressed the sweat-slicked hair.

"Forever?"

"Yeah, forever."

The salt of sweat and tears tasted sweet as Cavan's hungry mouth covered his. Fear of losing his lover and his lifestyle faded as the kiss deepened. He knew Cavan had a difficult road to travel, but he would be there for him every step of the way. Though Erik would never be forgotten, Cavan had healed Biton's broken heart. In return, he would see to his slave's wounded soul.

FOREVER

Chapter One

Cavan woke in a cold sweat. His heart beat a sharp pace in his ears. Terror tightened his chest. The sound of his master's steady breathing barely eased Cavan's fear.

Darkness cocooned them in Biton's wide bed. If only he could stay wrapped in the safety of his presence...

Red numbers glared at him from the clock on the nightstand. Just after midnight, he had been asleep for a couple of hours.

Biton had been tired when he got home. Tired and preoccupied. He hadn't discussed what was on his mind and a slave knew better than to ask questions. Anxiety accompanied his master's silent mood.

Biton Savakis was a different kind of master. Not like the one before. Master Wainwright would never have taken Cavan into his bed. Never wrapped comforting arms around him and simply fallen asleep. Wainwright would have taken what pleasure he required and locked Cavan in a stinking basement room with a blanket for a bed and a bucket for a toilet.

Cavan fingered the soft sheet covering him. The clean smell and cushioned mattress were a secret pleasure. And the man whose chest lined his back was his life. At least what he wanted out of life.

After four months of therapy and steady reassurance from Biton, Cavan still couldn't convince himself it wouldn't end soon.

"What's wrong?" A gentle hand slid across Cavan's chest.

"Nothing," Cavan lied. "Go back to sleep." At one time, lying to his master wouldn't have been possible. Now, he had to or risk losing the only good thing he remembered in his life.

A snuffling breath tickled the back of Cavan's neck. "You first." Biton's mumbling lips teased his shoulder.

Cavan turned his head toward Biton. Gentle kisses and a scratchy stubbled face contrasted against his jaw. "I didn't mean to wake you."

"It's okay." Arms encircled him and tightened. Biton's lips found his.

The now familiar tightness in his groin tingled. His cock filled as Biton's tongue slid across the seam of his mouth. A wandering hand helped with long languid strokes.

Biton's thickening cock rubbed against Cavan. Short gentle strokes pushed between his cheeks, plowing through the furrow of his ass.

"Nightmare?" Biton whispered.

Cavan nodded. One he had more often as Wainwright's trial approached. Four months ago, emboldened by Biton's support and reinforced by the need to obey his new master, Cavan accused Wainwright of murder. Now, even with Biton's support, the idea of facing the man who abused him for nine years became more terrifying each day.

"Want to talk about it?" Biton's hand slid away from Cavan's cock. His arm tightened around Cavan's waist.

"No... I don't remember it now..." Cavan bit his lip as soon as the lie slipped out. To distract his master from further questions, Cavan pressed back against the hard flesh nestled between his ass cheeks.

Biton squeezed him tight then his fingers trailed down his lower stomach. His hand grasped Cavan's cock again. Long strokes topped by his thumb rounding over the sensitive tip made Cavan gasp for air.

The heat of Biton's body chased away residual fear. When Cavan was with his master, the world didn't matter. The long days while Biton was at work gave Cavan too much time to think about the terror of his past and the uncertainty of his future. The sessions with Dr. Merten didn't help.

Reliving his years of abuse, by both his former master and his foster parents two days a week kept his memories sharp and painful.

When he first came to stay with Biton, his master

made him talk about his life, about Wainwright and about Mateo, the slave Wainwright had killed. Therapy was supposed to help Cavan return to a normal life. Except Cavan's idea of normal didn't meet Dr. Merten's standard. He understood that the people who abused him were wrong but Biton was different. However, her disapproval of Biton's lifestyle, of his position as Cavan's master, showed in every session.

She insisted his sessions were confidential and not even Biton had the right to know what was said. Since his master assured him Dr. Merten was the best in her field, he tried to obey her.

Biton insisted he continue even after Cavan made his choice to stay three months ago.

Although Biton said he could stay forever, his master hadn't drawn up a new contract and they hadn't been in the playroom since the last day of the old contract. He feared his master had changed his mind.

"I want you..." Biton's whispered words sent shivers through him.

If only those words meant more than sexual attraction... Cavan slid his hand behind him and over Biton's muscular hip. Pulling the firm ass toward him, he pushed back into the heat of his cock. "Take me... Just like this..."

Biton's hand scrambled under the pillow for the lube and condoms they kept there.

Cavan released his grip on Biton's ass. His master's warm body rolled away leaving a cool void. A plastic cap snapped open followed by the rip of the small packet. Cavan bit his lip in anticipation.

Cold slippery fingers prodded his anus. He relaxed his body and welcomed the intrusion. Three swift strokes only teased him and then disappeared. Biton's body heat returned to line his back. His thick flesh pushed against the ring of muscle guarding his entrance.

"Yes…" Cavan breathed the word as his passage filled with hot cock. His eyes rolled shut from the intense pleasure. His need for Biton went beyond sex. The intimate connection helped reassure him of Biton's desire.

With both of them on their sides, Biton's strokes were slow, drawing out the intense sensations.

Cavan's head lolled back against Biton's shoulder. Canting his face toward his master, he caught Biton's lips. Long deep kisses with a lazy tongue explored Cavan's mouth, matching the pace of Biton's strokes.

Biton's hand slid down Cavan's stomach to his aching cock. His mouth captured Cavan's moans as Biton's thumb and forefinger circled just below the crown.

Everything moved in slow motion, lips, tongue, hand, and cock. Tension built to a raging climax and Cavan fell apart with an orgasm so intense his body seemed to collapse in on itself.

Gasping for air, his fingers clutched Biton's arm. Tears blurred his vision. He pulled away from Biton's kiss. Biting his lips, he resisted the urge to shout his love for Biton.

Biton promised him forever but the contract still hadn't been made. Uncertainty of the future frightened him in ways his former master never could.

Cavan turned his face into the pillow and let the tears flow as Biton's cock emptied into him.

Still shaking from the intensity of his orgasm, Biton leaned over Cavan. He plucked several tissues from a box on the nightstand. First wiping his hand, he then cleaned Cavan with a gentle touch and took a cursory swipe at the remaining mess on the bed.

After tossing the tissues toward the trashcan next to the bed, Biton held the quaking body of his lover. "Are you okay?"

Cavan's trembling seemed more than the aftershocks of orgasm. More like the shaking sobs of tears.

"Yes…" The gulping sound confirmed Biton's suspicions.

"Talk to me. I want to help."

Cavan shook his head. His only defiance since three months ago, when he deliberately provoked Biton to punish him, was refusing to talk. Something for which Biton couldn't, wouldn't, punish him.

Instead, Biton held him close, stroking his wavy red hair until the sobs slowed and his breathing evened out.

Once again, Biton wondered whether his course of action was the right one. Following Dr. Merten's advice hadn't worked before and he didn't think it was working now. But therapy of any kind needed more than four months to work. Cavan was abused for nine years. He wouldn't heal over night.

Although he refused to avoid sexual contact with Cavan, he'd agreed to postpone any discussion of a permanent arrangement as well as any dominant play. She insisted either would hamper Cavan's recovery. She'd voiced her disapproval of their physical relationship as well. Her theory was that any physical relationship without his full understanding could be damaging. But Biton couldn't turn Cavan away.

With a gentle kiss on his sleeping lover's temple, Biton whispered, "I love you."

———

Cavan climbed out of the car in front of Dr. Merten's office. The tall skyscraper with huge cold lobby intimidated him. After four months he should be accustomed to the sight. At first, Biton brought him to his sessions and waited for him. Now that Biton had gone back to work fulltime, he arranged for a car service to carry him back and forth. The sessions seemed longer knowing Biton wasn't just beyond the door.

With a sigh, Cavan marched to the entrance and pushed through the revolving door. He kept his head down as he walked past the security guards in the lobby. As the only occupant of the elevator, he breathed a sigh of relief.

He'd begun to hate his therapy. A measure of distrust had for Dr. Merten crept into his mind over the last couple of months.

When the elevator opened, Cavan dragged his feet toward the therapist's office. Inhaling deep, he opened the door.

"Good afternoon!" The receptionist, Anita, always smiled.

Sometimes he wanted to ask her why she was always so happy but he didn't. He couldn't find the nerve to do more than respond. "Good afternoon." He hurried across the room to a corner chair as far away as he could get from her. A few times, she'd tried to talk to him. Her attempts made him nervous.

He ran his hands down the armrests before dropping them in his lap. The cold leather chairs reminded him of the sling in Biton's playroom. A shiver of memory, of his first time with Biton, warmed him.

"I'll let the doctor know you're here." She picked up the phone and punched a couple of numbers. "Mr. Delany's here." She paused to listen to Dr. Merten. "Yes, ma'am, I'll let him know." Hanging up the phone, she swiveled her chair in Cavan's direction. "She's running a little behind. She'll be with you in a minute."

He hoped she really meant a minute. Cavan studied the tips of his sneakers. It helped keep him from making eye contact. Although he tried, looking at people in the face was something he couldn't quite do yet without a surge of panic threatening. A slave wasn't supposed to be so bold. Only with Biton and sometimes Dr. Merten. Even then, the doctor's expressionless stare stirred something close to fear. The blank look was too close to Master Wainwright.

Biton told him the doctor would only do what's right for him. Cavan was supposed to trust her but trust wasn't a concept he could wrap his head around. Besides, he didn't like some of the things she said. Especially when she questioned Biton's motives for allowing Cavan to live with him.

The buzzing phone startled him.

"The doctor's ready to see you now." Anita's cheerful voice grated on his already tense nerves.

His inability to disobey forced him to his feet and toward the closed door.

———

Biton stared at the deposition in front of him but his mind was miles away. His partners begged him to return to work a month ago. With an overwhelming caseload, Biton had to choose between retiring to make way for another lawyer and going back to work.

Dr. Merten didn't see any harm in Cavan remaining alone at home. She believed it would help his self-confidence.

Still Biton hated leaving him to fend for himself on the days he had therapy. The car service delivered him door to door but he preferred to be with him. The sessions took so much out of his young lover. Being there to cheer him up, treat him to something special, when therapy was over had made a difference.

The buzzing intercom brought him out of his thoughts. He punched the speaker button with a little more force than necessary. "Yes." He winced at the shortness in his tone. "Sorry, Sharon. What's up?" No sense in taking his mood out on his secretary.

"Detective Casala and ADA Luca are here to see you."

"Send them in…" He wasn't expecting them. Mario Luca was handling the case against Wainwright. Having him show up unannounced wasn't a good sign.

Biton stood up and moved around the large wooden desk as the door opened. "Come in, gentlemen. What can I do for you?"

With lips drawn thin and a grim set to his dark eyes, Antonio grasped his hand tight. "There's been a *development*." He almost spit his disgust as he said the last word.

"What do you mean?" Biton glanced at Luca.

The assistant district attorney's gaze wouldn't meet his. "The District Attorney's office is considering a deal with Wainwright." The thin young man shook Biton's hand in a brief light grip.

A slight swell of hope lightened Biton's mood. If Wainwright pled out, Cavan wouldn't have to testify against him. The idea of facing his abuser terrified Cavan. But Antonio wouldn't be pissed if the deal were a decent one for the prosecution.

Biton motioned the two men toward the high-backed cushioned chairs facing his desk. As he walked around to the other side, he braced himself for the worst.

Luca exhaled a sharp sigh. "Look, the DA wants

the slave ring; Wainwright can deliver it. He's agreed to tell everything he knows—name names."

Easing into his chair, Biton kept his face passive. "For what?"

"A fucking walk…" Antonio interrupted before Luca could answer.

"Not a walk, Detective." Luca's guilty look hardened. "He'll get jail time." He ran his hand through his light brown hair.

"How much?" Biton asked. The flush of anger started before he heard the answer.

"The lowest the DA's willing to go is criminally negligent homicide." Luca's gaze darted down and focused on the nameplate on Biton's desk.

"One and half to four years?" A rush of anger swept through Biton. "For murder? For torturing someone to death?"

"Look, it's the best we can come up with and get the information we need. Forensics can't determine the exact cause of death. The only witness willing to testify is Mr. Delany."

A couple of seconds passed while Biton's mind processed Cavan's real name. "But he's a solid witness. And what about his assault?"

"Assault in the second degree, sentence to run concurrent." Luca evidently found his balls. His gaze met Biton's angry stare head on. "We have to stop the slave ring."

"How can you be sure his information is worth what you're giving away?" Biton ground out the words between clenched teeth.

"He can't," Antonio interjected. He straightened in his chair.

Luca sighed. "The deal won't be final until sentencing. We'll pull in every available investigator to work his leads until then. If something viable doesn't show up, the deal is dead. It's part of the agreement."

"When's the sentencing?"

"Six weeks."

As an attorney, an officer of the court, Biton understood the need to deal with scum like Wainwright. Considering the possible number of victimized children sold into sexual slavery and worse by this pedophile ring, the district attorney had no choice.

Biton had promised Cavan the man who put him through hell on earth would go away forever. How would he explain the meaning of this deal to his terrified lover? On the other hand, Cavan wouldn't be required to testify. Maybe he could put his ordeal behind him quicker if he didn't have to face his abuser in court.

Thoughts of his lover's fears brought his mind back to Cavan's therapy session. Glancing at the clock behind his guests, he noted Cavan should be at the doctor now.

"I wanted to be the one to inform you of the possible deal but I need to get back to the office now." Luca stood. "If you or Mr. Delany has any questions, feel free to contact me."

"Thank you." Biton shook his hand over his desk.

Antonio waited until the door closed behind the

assistant district attorney. "I'm sorry. I don't think it's right."

"As a defense attorney, I understand the need to deal, to put away the people responsible for Cavan's torture and who knows how many others but..." He stood staring out the window, his shoulders hunched over, hands in his pockets. Cars were tiny specks on the broad avenue below. "Do you think Wainwright has anything of real value?" Biton needed reassurance.

"I don't know. He claims that all his slaves came from the same source. If he's been doing business with them all these years, he should know something."

"I don't know how to explain this to Cavan." Biton scrubbed his face with the palms of his hands. "I promised him Wainwright would go away forever." Forever... The word echoed in his mind.

He'd also promised his wounded lover that he could stay with him forever. Cavan never mentioned it after that night. With Dr. Merten's warnings, Biton hadn't either. Maybe he should get the doctor's advice before telling Cavan.

Although Biton wasn't sure Dr. Merten was working out. Rather than improving, Cavan seemed to be more withdrawn than ever. He'd considered looking for another therapist to treat Cavan but meeting new people was difficult for the young man.

"Do you want me to talk to him with you?" Antonio turned to face him.

"No, thanks." Biton sighed and glanced at his watch. "He's still at Dr. Merten's. I'll cancel the car service and pick him up myself. Maybe the doctor should be handy when I tell him."

———

Cavan huddled on the couch across from Dr. Merten's chair. The thickly cushioned couch swallowed him. Maybe if he could make himself small enough, he'd disappear into the furniture. Several bookshelves lined one wall, filled with books. Cavan liked books. He wondered what kind of stories Dr. Merten read.

"Michael, something is bothering you. You should tell me about it."

He fought the automatic shudder at the sound of his real name. Only Dr. Merten and the man from the prosecutor's office insisted on using it. He didn't identify himself with the child that was Michael Delany.

"It's nothing."

"Why don't you let me be the judge of that?" She paused for a moment. "Michael, therapy doesn't work if you don't talk."

"I don't know what to say."

Her long fingernails tapped her notepad. "Do you regret having sex with Biton?"

Tightness threatened Cavan's throat. "No! Never."

"So you want to stay with him."

"Yes." Cavan pulled his legs up to his chest. He whispered, more to himself than the doctor, "I don't know if he wants me to."

"Why would you say that?" Dr. Merten leaned forward, her eyes narrowed.

Cavan glanced down, away from the intense interest in her gaze. "He…" His mouth went dry. "He hasn't written the contract yet."

"Has he explained why?"

Shaking his head, Cavan forced a swallow past the tight lump in his throat.

She settled back in her chair, almost a relieved look crossed her face. "Maybe he's changed his mind. You have to consider it. Three months ago, he offered to let you stay forever."

Cavan shook his head. As much as he wanted to deny her words, he couldn't. He'd thought the same thing too often. Panic gurgled through his stomach. "But why has he let me stay with him?"

"Why do you think?"

"Because he feels responsible for me." Cavan said the words aloud for the first time. It couldn't be true. "No, he loves me." He looked up at the doctor. "He makes love to me, lets me sleep in his bed. Why would he do that if he didn't love me?"

Her hard eyes didn't reflect the sad smile on her face. "Because men like Biton Savakis are accustomed to doing what they want. He uses people, dominates them, inflicts pain." She leaned forward in her chair. "Didn't he beat you?"

"But it wasn't the same." A different kind of shudder swept through him. The memory of the restraints binding his arms and feet, the sting of the paddle transforming to intense heat with each blow and the shimmer of emotion in Biton's eyes… Sexual desire swirled through his body. His voice dropped to a whisper. "I wanted it…him."

He did then and he did now, want Biton and the things he did that day.

"Michael, what are you thinking about?"

Bowing his head, he mumbled, "Nothing." He pulled his legs tight against his chest to hide his rising erection.

"You should think about finding your own way in life." She leaned forward again. "Get away from dependence on someone else. Away from a lifestyle you had no choice in."

Anger took the edge off his arousal. She had no right to tell him what to do. Biton said it was Cavan's choice and he'd made it. He wanted what Biton offered.

As fast as his fury hit, it dissipated. Biton offered but he didn't follow through. "I don't want to talk anymore." Cavan stood. His appointment was nowhere near over but he couldn't stay here any longer.

"Michael, we're not done. Sit down."

Her stern tone almost made him obey. Almost. "No." Cavan stalked toward the door.

"Michael!" The doctor stood, her arm out, finger pointing at the couch. "Michael, sit down."

He turned to look at her. Shaking his head, he repeated the one word he'd never learned to use. "No." Grabbing the doorknob, he yanked open the door. His pace sped up through the waiting room. Anita looked up from her desk, startled as he ran by.

Chapter Two

Cavan ran past the security desk in the lobby. He needed to get away from that office, that woman. All she ever talked about was how wrong it was to want Biton, to stay with him.

She didn't understand and she never would. He needed Biton. His body ached for him. He wanted to give Biton everything he asked for. The summer heat couldn't compare to the fire burning through his body at the idea of his master's touch.

The car wouldn't be here to pick him up for a while. Afraid Dr. Merten would follow him, Cavan ran down the street.

His heart pounded in his throat as he dodged people in the afternoon crowds. He avoided making eye contact.

An almost physical pain swept through him. The idea of leaving Biton caused an ache in his chest and

161

made breathing almost impossible. Tears stung his eyes and blurred his vision. The heat of the day and the efforts of his flight caused sweat to trickle down his forehead and neck. His simple cotton t-shirt clung to his back and underarms with moisture.

Too many people, too open. He needed some place to hide. He slowed in his flight.

Gasping for air, he glanced around, fast so no one would accuse him of making improper eye contact. His former master had beaten that rule into him early in his service.

After so many years inside darkened rooms and a basement cell, he wasn't comfortable with open spaces, especially outside.

A small alleyway to his right was empty of people. He darted through the narrow opening. Stopping behind a large trash bin, he leaned over, his hands clutching his knees and gasped for air. With each breath came the stench of rotting food and the rank smell of garbage. The sound of his rapid heart beat muted the clatter of passersby and traffic.

As a slave to Master Wainwright, he'd never exercised. His slender frame stayed that way from a lack of food.

With panic stealing his breath, Cavan wasn't in any kind of shape for running. His scalp itched with trickles of sweat. His shirt was soaked from the heat and exertion. As his breathing eased toward normal, his brain kicked back into gear.

Running away from the doctor's office wasn't smart.

He needed to go back, wait for the car service.

"But what if she's looking for me?" He hated his appointments. More and more, the urge to tell Biton the things she said overwhelmed him.

Dr. Merten told him not to talk to Biton about their sessions. Biton said Cavan needed to do what the doctor said. Confusion didn't help his conflicted mind.

"Can't go back. She doesn't understand." He'd talk to Biton…tell him everything. Somehow, the decision eased his panic.

Now, he needed to find his way back to the doctor's office. Straightening, he yanked the bottom of his t-shirt up and wiped the sweat from his face.

Approaching the opening of the alley, he paused. Which way did he come from? A tendril of fear returned. He'd never been out in the city alone. Only with Biton.

"Calm. Think." Something Biton had said sparked his memory.

He patted his back pocket. With a sigh of relief, he pulled out his wallet. Biton had bought it for him during one of their first shopping trips. Opening the center pouch, he looked at the crisp bills inside. Biton had put them there the day he'd bought the wallet. A small piece of paper nested against the money.

Pulling the paper out, he mumbled the address aloud. Biton's address.

Yellow cabs rushed through the traffic on the busy street in front of him. Another decision made, he shoved his wallet in his pocket and darted between passersby toward the curb.

———

Biton knew something was wrong the minute he walked into Dr. Merten's office.

The receptionist started from her chair. "Mr. Savakis! I'll get Dr. Merten for you." Instead of buzzing the intercom, she hurried to the office door. Without knocking, she yanked it open and disappeared inside.

Less than a minute later, Dr. Merten appeared. "Mr. Savakis, I don't know what came over Michael. He bolted from his session."

"Bolted?" Anger and confusion swelled. "You mean he's not here?"

"No, I left a message at your office. I thought you knew...that's why you were here." Her round face flushed as she wrung her hands together.

"What the hell happened?" Biton shook his head and held up a hand to forestall her explanation. "Never mind. Do you have any idea where he went?"

"We called security but he ran past them and headed north." She ran her fingers through her dark hair.

"You and I will discuss this later." Biton turned and exited the office. His heart was in his throat at the idea of Cavan lost in the mid-afternoon bustle of Manhattan. His lover barely kept his panic attacks under control when they were together. Alone, there was no telling how he'd react. If he was already upset enough to run away from the doctor...

Time seemed to stand still as he waited for the elevator to arrive at the first floor. Dr. Merten must have called the security station. The two guards almost stood at attention as he approached them.

Biton didn't waste any more time on preliminaries. "The red-head Dr. Merten called you about. Which way did he go when he left the building?"

The older of the two men responded. "He turned right, heading north up the avenue."

"He looked really upset," the younger man volunteered. "I called for him to stop but he didn't act like he even heard me."

His partner glared at him. "He was out the door before we could do anything."

Biton nodded and started toward the exit.

"I hope he's okay," the younger man said.

"Thank you." Biton pushed through the revolving door. The summer heat was cool compared to his anger and worry. Pulling his cell phone from the clip at his waist, he dialed Antonio.

"Casala," Antonio answered.

"Antonio, Cavan's missing."

"What?"

"When I got to the doctor's office, he'd left, upset over something in his session. Ran out and up the avenue. I'm following but I don't know where he would have gone."

"I'll put out a broadcast. He's a witness in a high profile murder. That's enough to waive any objections."

"Thanks." Biton's relief at Antonio's words was

small but it was something.

"Do you think he could find his way home?"

"I don't know. He has the address in his wallet as well as money. If he was panicked enough to run from Merten, I don't know if he'd remember it. Besides, half the time he doesn't remember to take his wallet with him."

"I'll send a unit to the apartment just in case."

"Good idea." Biton flipped his phone shut. He looked at the compact piece of technology. He hadn't thought to get Cavan a cell phone. His lover was never more than a few steps from a phone. After today, that would change. Now he had to find him.

Cavan hadn't been outside alone since his former master kicked him out. Someone had always been with him. Even the car service drivers were tipped extra to make sure he made it from the car to the building on his trips to the doctor.

Alone in the swarming pedestrian traffic would double whatever terror sent him fleeing from Dr. Merten.

Biton stalked up the avenue, his eyes peeled for the wavy red hair of his missing lover.

———

Many times, Cavan had seen Biton hail a cab. He'd even seen it on television before. He could barely look up at the flowing traffic but he stood straight with his arm in the air mimicking the memory of his master's pose. A blur of yellow screeched to a stop in front of him. His gaze focused on the cab company name.

Yanking the door open, he crawled in.

"Where to?" A heavyset woman in the front seat watched him through the rearview mirror.

"T...t...two." He glanced down at the paper clutched in his fingers. "Two...three..." His eyes closed as he tried to calm his breathing.

She turned her head to peer through the heavy plastic divider. "Is that the address, son?"

Cavan nodded.

Her fingers curled through a small opening. "Why don't you let me see it?"

With a gasp of relief, he pushed the paper into her fingers.

She pulled a pair of glasses out of a cup holder and glanced at it. "Got it." She hit a button on the meter and the red numbers started ticking upward. "I'll have you there in a few minutes." She twisted a knob on the dash. "Why don't you sit back and cool off? You look like you just ran a marathon."

"Th... thank you..."

"It's okay, sweetie. I have a kid who stutters. He finds talking to strangers hard, too."

Cavan sat back as cool air filled the back seat. He didn't bother to explain.

"He's in college now," she continued. "Never thought he'd get that far. Trouble, that one was. But what's a mother to do? You have to love them."

Did they? He wanted to ask her. Were mothers required to love their children? Cavan didn't remember his mother. Most of his childhood was a blur of faded images.

School, he remembered he liked school. And books. Biton bought him all kinds of books. The shelves in his room were overflowing. With Biton gone during the day, Cavan devoured everything he could get his hands on.

Instead of scolding him for reading too fast, Biton just bought him more books. His master said he was pleased at his progress, said he was reading at a twelfth grade level already. Some of the first books did seem too easy when he reread them.

His breathing had steadied into something close to normal.

The woman driver in front kept chattering about her kids, her husband. Her voice calmed him as much as Dr. Merten's unnerved him. Most women scared him. They were one more unknown in a world Cavan didn't understand. But this lady seemed okay.

After it made a sharp turn, the car slowed. "Here we are, sweetie."

Cavan smiled at what she called him.

"Now that's a nice smile." Her dark eyes crinkled in the rearview mirror. "You should try using it more often." When the car stopped, she punched the button on the meter. "That'll be eighteen twenty-five."

The apartment…home… His stomach roiled in a combination of fear and relief. The calm of the cab ride vanished. Money. Most of the time, Biton handle the money. He'd made Cavan pay for things sometimes, to get used to it, but Biton was always there to keep him from making a mistake.

Groping for his wallet, Cavan pulled the soft leather from his pocket. Opening it, he glanced at the money inside.

"Eighteen twenty-five," the woman repeated.

Snagging two of the bills from inside, he pushed them through the little hole in the divider. Yanking the door open, he scrambled out of the cool interior into the hot summer afternoon.

The driver's window slid down. "Sweetie, your change!"

Ignoring her words, Cavan ran for the apartment building. Inside the foyer, he pushed his hand into his sweat damp pocket for his keys.

The cab sat there for a few seconds and then pulled away. At least he gave her too much money instead of not enough.

A police car pulled up as the cab left and parked by the fire hydrant. Cavan was too upset to wonder why. He needed to get in the house. His stomach churned with turmoil.

He opened the security door then darted for the stairwell. Afraid to wait for the elevator, he ran the stairs two at a time.

Finally in front of Biton's apartment door, Cavan fumbled with his key. Dropping it, he crouched to pick it up. His stomach leaped and dove at the same time. He'd done it. Hailed a cab. Biton would probably be mad he'd paid too much.

He'd also be mad if Cavan threw up in the hallway.

Snagging the key, he fitted it to the lock. The security alarm beeped its warning as he opened the door. Cavan keyed the simple four-digit code to disarm the system. Slamming the door shut behind him, he ran for the bathroom. The sound of the phone ringing barely registered but he couldn't stop to see who was calling. The turmoil in his stomach wasn't in the mood to wait another second.

One step inside the bathroom, he spewed the remains of his lunch across the floor, hitting the soft rug in front of the vanity. Splatter speckled the cabinet and the side of the toilet.

He hunched over the commode for the second round. The bitter taste of bile clenched his stomach and forced a last gagging retch through his throat.

Kneeling on the floor with his cheek resting on the cool porcelain seat, he waited for his stomach to settle.

Worry pushed aside his relief at being back in his safe zone. If it were up to him, he'd never leave Biton's apartment. His master wouldn't let that happen. He insisted they go out to restaurants, the park, shopping, movies, even once, the zoo.

Cavan hadn't liked the zoo. The caged animals reminded him too much of his own captivity. He hadn't said anything to his master but he must have realized Cavan hadn't enjoyed the outing. Biton hadn't suggested it again.

The movies he liked. In a darkened theater, he could forget other people were near and lose himself in the movie.

But most of all, he loved being here, in Biton's apartment with his master's arms wrapped around him. And Dr. Merten told him he had to leave.

With his legs still trembling, he stood. The bathroom needed to be cleaned before Biton got home.

———

"Cavan, if you're there, pick up the phone." Biton kept the fear in his voice under control.

Cavan wouldn't answer the phone unless he knew it was Biton calling. He'd hoped his lover had found his way home somehow. Even if he had, would he be too upset or distracted to answer? He punched the off button on his mobile.

The heat broiled through Biton's suit. He wasn't exactly dressed for a search through the hot August heat. After stripping off his suit jacket, he paused to wipe his brow with his handkerchief and roll up the sleeves of his shirt. Continuing his search, he checked the small restaurants along the avenue as well as asking several street vendors. No sign of his lover anywhere.

Scrolling through his phone numbers, he called the number to his security company.

"ATA Security, how may I help you?"

"Yes, my name is Biton Savakis. I need to know the recent activity on my alarm system." He rattled off the coded access number to verify his identity.

"Just a moment while I check, sir."

Biton knew it was a long shot but he prayed Cavan

171

remembered his instructions on how to get home by himself.

"Sir, the alarm was set at two o'clock this afternoon and released ten minutes ago. Do you need me to go back further?"

"No," Biton exhaled a long sigh of relief. "Thank you."

"Do you need assistance at your residence?"

"No, everything is okay." He shut the phone as he stepped to the curb. He needed to get home now.

———

The lukewarm water beat down on Cavan's head and sluiced down his body. The heat of his running escape left him stinking with sweat and the too familiar smell of fear. His hands pressed against cool tiles, he knew he should get out of the comforting shower and start cooking something for dinner.

Learning to cook was not only fun but it, in some small way, repaid Biton for giving him a roof over his head. He carefully picked out recipes and put together a shopping list each week. His attempts always garnered praise from his master. Biton always complimented his efforts, even when the meals were really not that good.

"Cavan!" Biton's voice echoed through the apartment.

With a start, Cavan turned off the water. "In here, Master." He yanked open the shower door and grabbed a towel.

The bathroom door burst open. Strong arms

wrapped around his wet body as he stepped out of the shower.

"Thank God, you're okay."

Biton knew.

"Master, I'm sorry. I couldn't stay there any longer. I didn't mean to disobey. Please don't be angry." Tears welled in his eyes. If Biton were mad, he might make him leave.

"No, no... I'm not mad. Not at you." Biton's face dipped in Cavan's shoulder. Gentle kisses lined his collarbone.

"But I shouldn't have left. You said I'm supposed to wait for the car." His fingers curled into Biton's sweat damp shirt.

"It's okay. As long as you're safe." Biton's lips ran up Cavan's neck and sought his mouth.

Gentle pressure urged Cavan open. He could taste the salty traces of sweat on Biton's lips.

"I was worried. I didn't know where you were." Biton's arms tightened around him.

"I took a cab, like you told me."

Breathing grew difficult as Biton squeezed him harder. "Glad you remembered."

The need to confess wouldn't leave Cavan alone. "I think I paid too much."

A soft chuckle wasn't the response he expected. "Doesn't matter, as long as you made it home." Biton raised his head. His eyes twinkled with amusement. "Next time, just call me. I would have come and got you."

Cavan dipped his face down. "I... I was upset. I didn't think."

Biton's hand cupped his chin and tugged his head up. "We need to talk about why. What did Dr. Merten say to upset you?"

His master had never asked him a direct question about his therapy session. Biton's instructions were to obey Dr. Merten and the therapist told him not to discuss their sessions. How did he answer?

"She..." Fear roiled through his belly again. Biton told him he had to follow the doctor's advice. If Biton knew what she said, would Cavan have to leave? Biting his lower lip, he shook his head. He wanted to tell Biton everything but he couldn't force the words from his mouth.

"It's okay. We can talk later." Biton brushed his lips with a gentle kiss. "I need a shower and I can hear your stomach growling. Let me get cleaned up and we'll get something for dinner."

Relief eased his nausea. Cavan nodded. "I can cook something while you shower."

A grin split Biton's face. "Actually, I thought we could order take out and you could join me in the shower." He fingered the towel draped around Cavan's hips. "Seeing as you're already dressed appropriately."

Desire eased his remaining fear. Tendrils of delicious arousal wove through his body and filled his cock.

Biton's hands traced his spine. A flurry of kisses covered his face and neck. The towel circling his waist pulled free. Cool air swirled around his ass before

Biton's hands grasped his cheeks. Massaging fingers helped ease the aching muscles from his earlier run.

"Sound like a good idea?" Biton whispered against his ear.

"Yes, Master."

Cavan slid his hands between their bodies. His fingers flipped the buttons on Biton's shirt, opening it to reveal his broad muscular chest. He ran his nails through the thick chest hair then brushed the tight point of a nipple. A shiver vibrated through his fingertips.

His master's dark eyes were almost black with lust and a gentle smile graced his rugged face.

With a shrug, Biton's shirt slid down his arms. Still tucked into his waistband, the pale material hung loose against his dark slacks. His hands came back to rest on Cavan's shoulders. His thumbs teased the sides of his neck.

Leaning forward, Cavan traced a circle around Biton's nipple with his tongue. Over the last few months, Cavan had taken pleasure in learning the little things that turned his master on. The idea of finding ways to please someone was a concept Cavan didn't understand at first.

Master Wainwright only required obedience. He took his pleasure without waiting for someone to give it to him.

Closing his mouth around Biton's peaked nipple, Cavan almost smiled at the man's soft moan. His tongue flickered across the tiny hardened flesh. The sharp taste of sweat burst across his taste buds. The musky smell of Biton's skin sent a thrill of desire coursing through Cavan's body. His engorged cock twitched with the joy of fulfilling his master's needs.

Biton's hands kneaded Cavan's ass with hard purpose. The push and pull of flesh around his hole made him long for the feel of Biton's cock filling him.

Slipping a hand down the front of Biton's slacks, Cavan sought his master's length. The thick flesh was hot and heavy inside the confines of his clothes.

A soft groan encouraged his boldness. Biton's hips surged forward. His cock pushed through Cavan's grasp.

With a final lick and suckle to the taut nipple, Cavan slid to his knees at Biton's feet. His fingers made short work of Biton's belt and fly. Pulling the soft material of his briefs away from his leaking flesh, Cavan licked the glistening crown.

The ripe smell of sweaty musk only served to arouse Cavan more. He closed one hand around his own flesh while the other guided his master's into his mouth.

"Oh, God, Cavan!" Biton's hands fondled Cavan's hair. His hips bucked toward Cavan's willing mouth.

Holding his cock tight to keep from coming, Cavan welcomed the salty bitter taste of his master's juices. The hard flesh slid over his tongue into the back of his throat. Years of forced practice allowed him to take his master deep.

"Too much…" Biton moaned.

Cavan sucked hard to keep him from pulling out.

His own moan was of disappointment over the loss of the hard cock.

Hands caught him under his arms and dragged him to his feet. Warm kisses lined his face.

"Not yet, love. You're too good at that. I want to last longer than a few minutes."

The backwards praise delighted Cavan. He wrapped his arms around Biton. The brush of hard flesh against his erection heated his skin. Hearing Biton call him 'love' always sent a soft flutter of joy through him.

The term gave him a sense of belonging he'd never known. It also gave him hope that he was here, with Biton, for reasons other than a sense of responsibility on his master's part. The shudder that shook him wasn't just arousal. His session with Dr. Merten intruded on the rapture he felt in Biton's embrace.

"Let's get in the shower." The whispered words brought him back.

He released Biton. After helping him out of the rest of his clothes, he followed his master into the large shower.

The large square cubicle was more than big enough for two. Three showerheads lined two of the three walls. Biton only turned on one set, leaving part of the shower free from the spray.

Water drenched Cavan from head to foot. Opening his mouth, he caught the spray on his tongue. He stood in the middle imagining he was standing in a rainstorm. He loved this shower. Master Wainwright allowed his slaves to bathe, demanded they keep clean, but the bathroom they used had a simple tub, no shower. He didn't remember showers when he was younger. The first time he'd taken one here, he'd been bowled over by the sensation.

Biton moved behind him. His cock nestled in the crack of Cavan's ass. "I was worried about you." His arms tightened around Cavan, pulling him closer.

"I was scared but I remembered what you said. About my wallet."

"And a cab."

Cavan nodded. "I couldn't talk to the woman. I gave her the paper and she brought me here."

"I'm glad."

"I didn't feel good. I was afraid I was going to be sick so when she told me the amount, I gave her two of the bills in my wallet." Cavan waited for Biton's anger.

Instead of scolding, Biton kissed the side of his neck. "It was worth forty dollars to have you home safe."

Home… This was his home. The first he could remember. Other places were just houses with people who wanted to hurt or use him. Tears stung his eyes at the idea of leaving.

Biton's hand slid up his chest to his face. A soft tug on his chin urged him to turn toward the gentle mouth teasing his neck.

He welcomed the warm kisses, wet from the spray of water. Turning within the circle of Biton's arms, he opened to an insistent tongue. Water sheered down his back, seeping over his shoulders and slicking the contact between their bodies.

Hands grasped his ass, pulling his cheeks apart. Warm water teased his hole. Fingers followed, circling the ring of sensitive nerves.

"I want you." Cavan's whisper caused Biton's hands to clutch his ass.

For reasons Cavan couldn't understand, voicing his desires increased his master's passion. That knowledge was the only thing that would make Cavan bold enough to speak, even if the words were true.

"Turn around." Biton's tone was somehow soft and commanding at the same time. His hands urged Cavan toward the wall.

Cavan didn't hesitate and obeyed without another word. Splaying his hands against the water-warmed tiles, he spread his legs.

Teasing fingers ran down his spine followed by warm kisses. Biton's arm wrapped around his waist. His hand grasped Cavan's aching cock. His other hand slipped between Cavan's legs from behind. "Further apart." Fingers tapped against his inner thigh.

Shuffling his feet, he obeyed. With his legs wide open, water once again teased his hole.

"Stay just like this. Don't move," Biton whispered against Cavan's ear.

Cavan froze, almost holding his breath. His heart thudded in his chest. Anticipation with Biton always ended in more pleasure than Cavan thought possible. Unlike his past life, when waiting was filled with the fear of guaranteed pain.

SHAYLA KERSTEN

Biton's hand pulled away from Cavan's aching cock. Fingers traced his spine from his neck to the dip at the top of his ass. Hungry kisses followed, sucking water from Cavan's skin.

When Biton's mouth reached his ass, Cavan flexed back toward his master's touch.

Sharp teeth nipped the fleshy middle of his left butt cheek. "Don't move." Thumbs dug into the crack of his ass, parting his cheeks.

Cavan's muscles tightened but he didn't move.

Biton's tongue fluttered across the sensitive nerves surrounding his hole. Cavan gasped for air. His head drooped forward. His forehead rested on the tiles. He bit his lower lip as a moan vibrated through his throat.

Kissing lips joined the flickering tongue. Cavan resisted the need to press back. His fingers curled into fists against the wall.

A wet finger pushed into him. Licks and kisses continued around the outer ring. Biton pushed deeper, curling his finger.

Cavan couldn't stop a yell when Biton pressed against his prostate. The hard knot of nerves sent fire through his balls and his aching cock. A small spurt of cum drizzled down his length.

"What do you want, Cavan?" Kisses spread left across his buttock. Nipping teeth scattered tiny jolts of pleasure.

"I want you inside me." The words blasted out in a rush.

Biton rose from the floor of the shower. His lips

retraced his journey up Cavan's spine. With a final stroke of Cavan's prostate, Biton slid his finger out of him.

Out of the corner of his eye, Cavan saw Biton reaching for a small shelf in the corner of the shower. Among the containers of soap and shampoo hid a bottle of lube and several condoms. "Yes…" He couldn't stop the anxious plea. He needed the feel of Biton's cock, his flesh filling him. He needed what came next.

Frantic kisses along his shoulder and the snap of the plastic cap answered his whispered word. Slippery fingers teased his hole.

"Hurry, please…"

Pushing past the ring of muscle, Biton's finger curved once again into his prostate. A shudder of pleasure threatened to buckle his knees. Another finger slid beside the first. The accustomed burn of stretching only signaled the coming ecstasy.

"More…"

"I love to hear you like this," Biton whispered near Cavan's ear. "Begging, needing… Ask me for what you want."

"Please. Master. Fuck me."

Biton's fingers punctuated his whispered words. "Say it again. Louder."

"Fuck me!" His whispers graduated to a groan. Again, the hard strokes sent shudders through him.

"Louder!"

The stern command nearly sent Cavan over the edge. "Fuck me, Master."

His yell prompted the loss of Biton's fingers.

"Fuck me!" The shout mingled with a sob. "Please, Master." His fingers tried to curl into the solid wall. His body shook with anticipation. Knees threatened to fail him.

The blunt head of Biton's cock pushed against his hole. Cavan forced his muscles to relax, to take the hot flesh into him.

"Please fuck me." The reward for his final shout slammed into him, filling him completely. A second stroke, as hard as the first, nailed his prostate. Nothing could have stopped him from coming unglued.

His seed spurted against the shower wall. Stray sprays of water mixed with the thick white fluid, streaking it down the tiles.

Biton moaned against his shoulder. His strokes became frantic, erratic. "Oh, God…" His groan ended when his teeth sank into hard muscle.

Cavan knew he'd bruise from the bite but he didn't care. The only thing that mattered was Biton's pleasure. He was more than willing to suffer any pain his master gave him for the intense pleasure coursing through his body.

A surge of emotion threatened to escape as a sob. He wanted this, his master's touch, his kisses. He needed to give him everything he wanted or desired. To return everything given to him and more. How could he make Biton understand?

Chapter Three

Biton's arms caught Cavan's weight as his lover's knees gave out. He lowered him to the shower floor. Water caught the wall Cavan's body had sheltered. The evidence of his pleasure washed away.

His mind had trouble grasping the fact that Cavan had come without having his cock touched. Not an easy thing for any man to do but Cavan was desensitized to sex after so many years of abuse. Biton would have thought it impossible.

Was it just the angle? The way Biton ordered him around? Or was it relief from the fright he'd been through this afternoon? Whatever the cause, Biton was determined to find out. A twinge from his expended cock accompanied hope. If Cavan got off from the way Biton ordered him around, there was hope his lover might actually learn to enjoy the play Biton craved.

He was already resigned to end most of the lifestyle

he'd lived for the last twenty years if it was the only way to heal Cavan and keep him in his life. His lover's natural submissiveness would probably always be there and that was some consolation. If there could be more, even in small increments…

"You okay?" he whispered.

Cavan nodded but his body shook with more than the aftermath of an orgasm.

"Hey, what's wrong?" Biton reached up and shut off the shower. "Talk to me."

"I can't…" A sob choked his words.

"Why not?" Stroking Cavan's hair, he tightened the arm around his waist.

"You…said to do…what the doctor said…" The gasping words didn't make sense.

"Yes, but why can't you talk to me, tell me what's bothering you?"

"She said not to…"

"Not to talk to me?" Biton didn't understand but in a way, it explained Cavan's increasing depression and withdrawn attitude. "Love, you can tell me anything you want. It doesn't matter what."

"But you said to do what she said." Cavan wiggled around to face Biton. His green eyes were brilliant in his misery.

"I don't understand why she wouldn't want you to talk to me. Maybe she meant you shouldn't if it made you uncomfortable. I haven't asked because I didn't want to put you in the position of feeling like you had to obey and tell me." Biton kissed the frown wrinkles creasing Cavan's forehead. "A relationship has to be based on communication or it won't work."

"Like in the playroom." Cavan's throat worked hard against his Adam's apple. "When you said I had to tell you if I wanted something or not."

"Exactly." A shiver of pleasure curled through Biton's stomach and headed straight for his balls. The memory of that night three months ago was still fresh in his mind. "It can't just be in the playroom. It has to be in our everyday life. If something is wrong, you need to tell me."

The chill of the air conditioning chased away the residual warmth from the shower. Goosebumps formed along Cavan's wet skin.

"Let me finish my shower. You get dressed and call for some food. Then we'll talk. Okay?"

"Which food?"

Biton planted a quick kiss on Cavan's mouth. "By now, you know what I like from any of the menus in the kitchen. You pick. Surprise me."

The worried frown faded, replaced by a look of intense concentration.

Biton stood then pulled Cavan up from the shower floor. "Go." He swatted a wet ass cheek for good measure.

His lover's startled grin contained only pleasure and, maybe, promise. Cavan opened the shower door enough to slip out. Through the clear glass, Biton watched him wrap a towel around his body before he turned on the water again.

Between the scare this afternoon and now worry over the doctor's warnings, how was he supposed to tell Cavan about the DA's deal with Wainwright?

As he lathered his hair, he mused over what Cavan had said about Dr. Merten not wanting him to talk. It just didn't make sense. Talking was the point of therapy, even if it wasn't to the doctor. Cavan had to have misunderstood.

They would talk tonight about Dr. Merten and what was bugging Cavan. He'd wait until morning to tell him Luca's information.

He'd been looking forward to a relaxing weekend. His work had kept him tied up in knots for the last few days. One of his clients was accused of murder, with no alibi and too much circumstantial evidence. Fortunately, this morning, the police discovered hard forensics pointing to someone else and the charges were dropped.

So instead of a calm weekend with his lover, he had only more turmoil.

His curiosity over Cavan's issues urged him to hurry through the rest of his shower.

—

Biton dressed in a pair of gym shorts and a t-shirt. Brushing his damp hair back, he went in search of his lover.

Seated at the dining room table, Cavan stared at an empty plate in front of him.

"What did you order?"

"Chinese." His gaze flickered up at Biton. "I can call and cancel it," he added in a rush of words.

"Chinese is fine. I trust your choices." Biton caressed the back of Cavan's neck. "I trust you." He ran his hand down Cavan's arm then tugged at his hand. "Come on. Let's go sit on the couch while we wait for the food."

Cavan trailed behind him, his feet dragging. Normally, Cavan enjoyed cuddling.

Biton plopped down into the soft cushions pulling his hesitant lover with him. "Cavan, you can tell me anything you want. About your sessions, about what happened today, anything. It's called conversation. You don't have to get permission from me or anyone else." He hugged Cavan close. "We're lovers, we're partners. Talking about our day, about things bothering us, is something we have to do to stay together. Holding back creates problems."

"I want to stay with you." Cavan buried his face in Biton's neck. "Please don't make me leave." Panic tinged his voice.

"You don't have to. Why would you think that?" Biton hugged him close. "I don't want you to go anywhere."

"Dr. Merten says I need to leave and you said I should do what she told me..."

Biton's blood began a slow burn toward anger. "Why would she say that?" Maybe Cavan misunderstood.

"She says I'm too dependent on you. I need to learn to do things for myself." The muffled voice was calmer.

"You are learning to do things for yourself here. Did you tell her that?"

"I am?" Cavan's head popped up from its hiding place.

Biton laughed at the confused expression. "Yes, you read magazines and books, you cook, you do the shopping lists, you do the laundry and keep the house clean. You even took a cab home today all by yourself." He planted a kiss on the soft lips pursed with uncertainty. "You've mastered the remote control and the telephone. You've gotten very good at computer games." He grinned at the sheepish look that flashed across Cavan's face. "None of this may seem like much to her, but I think you've made great strides in the last few months. Remember what you were like when you first came here."

"I guess…"

"I don't guess—I know. You've even learned to voice your needs when it comes to sex."

A flush of red started across Cavan's face.

Biton pressed his mouth against Cavan's ear. "If it weren't for good soundproofing, the neighbors would know you want me to fuck you," he whispered.

Cavan ducked his head again but the bright red tinge on his ears gave away his embarrassment.

"Don't be ashamed. I love it when you tell me what you want."

A mumble vibrated on Biton's neck but he couldn't understand the words. "What did you say?"

"What if I want…" The last few words trailed off

too low to hear.

"Cavan, I can't understand you." He shrugged away from Cavan then reached for his face. Cupping his cheek, he asked again, "What did you say?"

With his eyes closed, Cavan whispered, "What if I want to go to the playroom?"

Biton couldn't stop the sharp intake of air anymore than he could keep his blood from rushing south.

Cavan's eyes popped open. His gaze combined fear and arousal in equal measures. "But Dr. Merten says it's wrong to want someone to hurt you."

The doorbell picked the worst possible moment to ring.

"Damn!" Biton didn't want to stop the conversation just yet. "Let me get the food and then we'll talk some more."

Cavan nodded and pulled away from Biton. He curled in the corner of the couch, doing his making-himself-small routine.

For someone who had never had a sense of self, Cavan's body language was very expressive. Maybe because he never learned deceit or guile.

Biton buzzed the deliveryman in downstairs before going to the bedroom for his wallet. Tonight was not going to be the night to tell Cavan about Wainwright. Too many other things needed to be discussed.

The doorbell ringing again signaled the arrival of dinner. Biton hurried to the front door.

Biton didn't have much of an appetite and it seemed neither did Cavan. The younger man toyed with the food on his plate, rearranging more than he ate.

"Okay, seems as if neither of us is hungry right now." Biton thought they could talk over dinner but Cavan had withdrawn once the food arrived.

Cavan darted a glance Biton's direction before his gaze refocused on his plate. Pushing his fork through some fried rice, he lifted it toward his mouth. Once again, his eyes cut toward Biton.

The grin splitting Biton's face must have triggered Cavan's amusement. A smile spread across his lips as he set the fork back on the plate.

"You don't have to eat if you're not hungry." To emphasize his words, Biton pushed his own plate away.

Cavan mimicked his action. "I got sick earlier. My stomach doesn't feel too good."

"Sick?" He reached across the corner of the table separating them and rested his hand on Cavan's forehead. "Are you coming down with something?" His skin was cool to the touch.

"No." Cavan shook his head. Once again, he lowered his gaze. "When I got home…my stomach felt bad."

Biton ruffled the curly red hair. "Nerves."

A slight flush accompanied Cavan's nod.

"Nothing to be embarrassed about. Happens to everyone at some time or another." Biton pulled away and began closing the containers of food. "Let's put this away. You may be hungry later."

Cavan's hands followed Biton's lead. As he stood up, holding two of the containers, he asked, "Everyone? Even you?"

"Yes." Biton chuckled as he grabbed two containers by the wire handles in one hand. The other hand snagged his plate. "I've had the feeling before; and thrown up. But you get used to the sensation and learn to control it instead of letting it control you."

"What made you get sick?" Cavan followed Biton into the kitchen.

"My first day in court as lead attorney. It wasn't even an important case. Routine almost, but I had butterflies so bad I thought I would fly away."

"Did you throw up in court?" Cavan's eyes were round with astonishment.

Biton laughed. "No, though I wasn't sure I'd make it through my opening statements. I managed to make it to the men's room." He set the dishes and Chinese food boxes on the counter. "So see, there's nothing to be ashamed of. Many people have had the same feeling and for a lot less reason."

"I didn't really make it." One side of Cavan's mouth curled in a wince. "The bathroom rug is in the washing machine."

Biton relieved Cavan of the food he carried. "Ah, but you took care of it. That sounds like being self-sufficient."

A frown creased Cavan's forehead. He drew a deep breath. "It does, doesn't it?" His face blossomed in a radiant smile.

Wrapping his arms around Cavan, Biton planted a quick kiss on his mouth. "See, talking with me can help too. I don't know why Dr. Merten didn't think it was a good idea. Talking things over strengthens any relationship, between friends, family or lovers. Asking questions about things bothering you helps clear up misunderstandings before they go too far." He pulled Cavan tight against him. "I don't want you to be afraid of me or scared to ask me anything."

"Do you love me?" The words were a faint whisper.

"Yes, of course, I do." What prompted this? Biton tried to show him in everything he did.

"You don't say it." Cavan's face retreated into Biton's neck.

He shook his head at his own stupidity. "Cavan, I love you. I forget things like that. Erik and I were together for so long. We understood each other, the way we felt. We expressed it in actions, not so much in words." He kissed the side of Cavan's neck. "I guess I forget things are different now."

"You still miss him?" This time Cavan raised his head to meet Biton's gaze.

"Yes. I do." His throat tightened at the memory of his deceased lover. "I always will. We were together for a long time. But I'm happy you're here with me and my past doesn't change how I feel about you."

"But you and Erik used the playroom."

Biton nodded slowly. "Yes, we did. Not all the time. More like special treats, never so much that it became routine. And always when we both wanted it."

192

"Do you want that with me?" Cavan swallowed the last word but maintained eye contact.

"Yes." Biton smiled. "I do. Very much." Even now, his cock filled with excitement at the idea. He pressed against Cavan to let him feel how much. "But only when you understand your limits. I don't want to hurt you."

Cavan's teeth worried his lower lip. "How will I learn my limits if we don't do anything?"

A laugh erupted from Biton. "You're right. I guess I hadn't thought about it that way." His hands ran down Cavan's back then up again. "The most important part of play is trust. You have to trust me to go only as far as you can handle. I have to trust you to tell me to stop if I go too far." Biton held his breath waiting for Cavan's response. The ache in his groin escalated. The idea of Cavan submitting, willingly, to a scene, even a mild one, sent tendrils of need through his lower stomach, curling into his balls.

"I want to." Cavan's voice trembled but his jaw locked in determination.

Biton exhaled a long breath. "Okay." His arms clenched around Cavan. "Okay."

Chapter Four

Biton stood behind Cavan in the doorway to his private dungeon. The familiar scent of leather invaded his lungs. His playroom was well equipped. Money had its advantages. Most of the equipment he'd installed himself, with Erik's help.

The pillory they'd used before stood in one corner of the room. Opposite it was a large leather sling. The other corners had a St. Andrew's cross and bondage table. Hanging from the center of the room was a series of sturdy hooks, placed strategically for suspension. Four square pillars set off the center of the room. With heavy metal hitching rings on all sides, the pillars could double as whipping posts or be used in conjunction with the ceiling hooks. A dresser against one wall contained a variety of sex toys and small implements. Whips, paddles and chains of various strengths lined the wall near the dresser.

Watching Cavan for any sign of panic, Biton ushered him into the room. "You can change your mind." He slid his arms around Cavan. One hand slipped down Cavan's stomach to his groin. The hard bulge inside his jeans was a good sign.

Cavan shook his head. "I won't."

One fantasy of many replayed through Biton's mind. He left Cavan standing inside the door and walked to the dresser. Pulling the bottom drawer, he reached in for a set of suspension cuffs.

The elaborate configuration had a standard leather cuff with strong thick leather straps attached to the sides. A horizontal padded bar, at palm length away from the wrist, was secured between two sides of the strap. The center of the thick leather strap met in a point at the top and had a ring secured through it. He fingered the supple leather while he checked the bolts and latches for wear.

He pocketed a small bottle of lube and a couple of condoms.

Turning back to Cavan, he caught his slave's hungry look before his eyes cast down. "Take off your shirt, shoes and socks but leave your jeans."

Cavan didn't hesitate. His clothes dropped to the floor next to him.

"Come here."

When Cavan stopped in front of him, he kept his gaze down.

"In here, the rules are different. Anywhere else in the apartment or when we're out, you can speak to me

195

when you want. You can call me by my name. But in here, you speak when I say you can unless you need me to stop. You always refer to me as Master or Sir."

Cavan nodded. A slight tremble shivered through his slender frame.

"Are you scared?"

At first, his head moved from side to side but then changed to another nod.

Biton caressed his cheek. "I'll stop when you want me to. You remember the safe words."

"Yes, Master."

"Someday, we won't need them. When our trust in each other is perfect, safe words won't mean anything. Until then, you'll always have a way to stop me." Biton held up the cuffs. "Hold out your hands."

Cavan complied. He was trembling as Biton fastened the soft leather around his wrists but he stayed silent. His fingers curled around the padded bar.

Tugging on the ring of one cuff, Biton led his silent slave to the center of the room. A small step stool was off to one side. He snagged it with his foot and positioned it under the two hooks spaced about two feet apart. The open ends of the hooks were close to the ceiling, a little more than the thickness of the rings on the cuffs.

He pointed to the step stool. "Get up there and slip each of these rings over one of those hooks." He pulled at the solid ring and glanced at the ceiling.

Cavan's only reaction was to obey. Clothed in just his jeans, Cavan stood waiting, his fingers fondling the cuffs' crossbars.

"I'm going to remove the stool. I want you to put your weight on the bars so you don't jerk when I pull it away."

His hands tightened on the bars. The muscles in his arms bulged.

When Biton bent over to move the stool, Cavan lifted his feet off the wooden step.

"Now relax into a hanging position."

Slowly his muscles eased in his arms and his body hung from the restraints. Only Cavan's toes brushed the floor. Enough maybe to steady him, but not enough to hold his weight. Erik had been shorter than Cavan. His feet hadn't touched at all.

Biton's already engorged cock ached with need at the sight.

A slight sheen of sweat already coated the tight muscles across Cavan's chest. His eyes fluttered back and forth beneath his lowered eyelids. His erection strained against the front of his jeans. Gravity pulled the blue denim down far enough that the head of his glistening cock protruded at the waistline.

"You're beautiful like this," Biton whispered. He traced a line down the inside of Cavan's arm, across the soft damp fur of his armpit. He shifted directions and crossed Cavan's chest to a hard nipple. A teasing circle ended in a sharp pinch.

Cavan moaned but he strained to push his chest toward Biton.

"You like that?" A swift pinch to the other side.

"Yes, Master."

Crossing the room, Biton opened another dresser drawer. Grabbing a pair of clamps, he returned to Cavan.

Leaning forward, he licked Cavan's right nipple.

Cavan tried again to push into the sensation. His body swung gently.

Biton steadied him. The gentle lick turned to a hard suck, working the nub of flesh to a sharp point. His teeth caught it and bit, not hard but enough to garner a gasp from Cavan.

With the tiny morsel warmed up, Biton slipped on a nipple clamp.

Cavan's body jerked but he didn't try to move again.

Making quick work of the other nipple, Biton stepped back to admire his handiwork.

Beads of sweat had replaced the soft shine. The silver chain hanging between the nipple clamps swayed with each panted breath. Muscles stood out all along Cavan's upper body. The strain of hanging could be intense but so far, Cavan hadn't complained.

Biton leaned over and licked a bead of pre-cum from the tip of Cavan's confined cock. A gasping moan rewarded his efforts.

He massaged the hard flesh through Cavan's jeans. His fingers worked up and down the rigid length. Cavan's toes scrabbled for limited hold on the floor. Reaching lower, he cupped Cavan's balls, rolling his sac through the denim.

"So incredible…" Biton murmured. His hand

moved up to the waist of Cavan's jeans. His fingers dipped into the waistband and squeezed the head of Cavan's cock.

Cavan's teeth dug into his lower lip but a groan still escaped.

Biton released his cock and pulled the button free. His fingernail ran down the zipper and back up again. Tugging Cavan's fly open, his smile widened.

Cavan hadn't worn underwear. His thick cock sprang from the confining jeans.

Wrapping a hand around the hot flesh, Biton stroked it several times.

Moans were Cavan's only response.

Pleased with his behavior, Biton rewarded him by suckling the tip of his cock. His hand ran up the taut stomach. Fingers tugged at the thin chain connecting the two nipple clamps.

A soft gasp escaped Cavan's open mouth. His breathing settled into a steady pant.

Biton peeled Cavan's jeans down his legs. Leaning over, he tugged the bunched clothing off Cavan's feet. Eye level with the leaking cock, Biton ran his tongue around the crown. The bittersweet taste of his slave's juices teased his mouth.

The hot flesh was too much temptation. Sucking half Cavan's length into his mouth, his hand reached below and found the tight balls. Cavan's body jerked but the only sound he made was a whimper.

He couldn't leave Cavan hanging long. His muscles weren't accustomed to the strain. It would take many sessions to build up to any length of time.

Didn't matter. The need for release was almost painful.

Standing in front of Cavan, he stripped his t-shirt over his head. With a quick tug, the loose cotton gym shorts fell to the floor.

"I'm going to fuck you just like this." He pulled the hard flesh standing at attention. "You want that?"

Cavan nodded. Sweat drizzled down his face. His gaze met Biton's for the first time since they entered the room. Half-lidded and almost sleepy with lust, his green eyes were darker than normal. His mouth hung open. Rapid breath panted past his lips.

"Tell me what you want."

"Use me, Master. Fuck me." Cavan's gaze didn't drop. His nostrils flared with each breath. "Fill me with your cock."

It was Biton's turn to gasp. Cavan's sincerity and arousal gave him hope again. Cavan wanted this as much as he did. Maybe for the wrong reasons but the hard weeping cock couldn't be faked.

Cavan's gaze wavered and his eyes lowered.

Reaching for his discarded shorts, Biton retrieved the lube and a condom from the pocket. He walked around Cavan while he opened the lube. A few quick strokes pushed the slippery gel deep into Cavan's hole. Not much resistance since only a couple of hours had passed since their shower.

He ripped open the condom and sheathed his cock. The slight friction of his own hand caused his balls to tighten. As he walked around to face his lover, he slicked his cock with the cold lube. He stopped in front of Cavan's flushed body.

"Cavan, wrap your legs around my waist." He tugged at Cavan's thighs to emphasize his words.

The long limbs trembled as he obeyed. Biton's cock slid into the crack of Cavan's ass.

"Ease your weight into me."

A small sigh accompanied the burden.

Biton grimaced. Cavan may have reached his limit. "Are you okay?" The slight hesitation prompted Biton to continue. "Remember, we have to trust each other. If you need to stop, you have to tell me."

Cavan took a deep breath. "Not yet. Almost."

While kissing Cavan's sweat slick chest, Biton reached around the slim hips straddling him. Grasping his cock, he guided his aching flesh into the tight hole. The crown caught then slipped.

Cavan's moan merged with Biton's grunt.

He tried again. This time, he found his mark. With a sigh of relief, Biton slid into the silky passage. As much as he wanted to take his time, concern for Cavan's wellbeing combined with his own aching need decided his actions.

Flexing his knees, he pumped into the heat of his lover's ass. Hard pounding strokes meant to bring him to climax fast.

Lines of tension swept through his body, pooling low in his groin. The sweet heat engulfing his cock beckoned for his release. His balls pulled tight against his body. A flood of pleasure erupted, taking his breath, his coordination and his seed.

Cavan's body shook from strain and effort. Sweat slicked his skin, but not cum. Still hard, his cock strained between their bodies.

"Reach up and pull the cuffs off the hooks." Biton eased his cock out of Cavan and braced his legs for the rest of Cavan's weight. His lover didn't weigh much but the aftershock of his climax had Biton's knees still quaking.

Cavan's arms dropped around Biton's neck. Maintaining a firm grasp on Cavan's ass, Biton carried his burden to the bondage table. He eased his lover on the edge of the padded vinyl table.

"Lay down," he whispered. "Relax your muscles."

Cavan stretched out on the padding. His arms trembled as he tried to find a way to settle the restraints beside him on the narrow table.

"Here." Biton pulled the release on each of the cuffs. He dropped the restraints and bar on the floor. "You did so well." His hands rubbed the tense arm muscles. Sweat acted as a lubricant. Leaning over his lips captured Cavan's. "So very good."

One hand slid up Cavan's arm then down his chest. He paused to remove the nipple clamps. Kissing a line down Cavan's throat, he soothed the pinched flesh with his tongue, first one side and then the other.

Cavan whimpered at his touch.

Moving down Cavan's torso, he lapped the salty sweat pooled in his navel. Cavan's back arched, pushing his stomach hard against Biton's face.

"A little sensitive there, eh?"

"Yes…" A shaking hand settled on Biton's head. Fingers combed through his hair. "Master," Cavan added.

Biton's fingers traced a line through Cavan's neatly trimmed public hair, avoiding his straining cock. "You didn't come."

"Last time I had to wait until you said I could."

"Hmmm. That's true." He ran a finger up the underside of Cavan's hard length. "Do you want to come?"

"Yes, Master." His hips undulated up. "Please may I come?"

"Yes, you may." Biton leaned over and sucked the leaking cock into his mouth. With fast bobbing strokes, he took Cavan's flesh deeper each time. It didn't take long before Cavan's bitter taste filled his mouth.

"Yes, Master!" Sobs mingled with Cavan's words. His fingers tangled in Biton's hair.

Biton released the softening flesh and moved up Cavan's body, fluttering kisses along the way. When he reached Cavan's lips, he devoured them, hungry for his lover's taste.

The tears streaming down Cavan's face slowed. His arms wrapped around Biton's neck in a loose embrace.

His kisses slowed. Pressing his forehead against Cavan's, Biton whispered, "We need to get you into a hot bath. It'll help ease the muscle strain."

Cavan lay back in the warm water. His neck and shoulders ached more than his arms. The huge bathtub, big enough for two, shot jets of water against Cavan's back and sides. Tonight hadn't been the first time he'd been suspended from a ceiling. Those times ended with being thrown back in his cell, not a long hot bath.

Biton circled past the bathroom door every few minutes to check on him.

His eyes drooped shut for the fourth time. It would be so easy to fall asleep here.

"Are you about ready to get out?" Biton's voice asked from somewhere above him.

Cavan nodded. His eyelids almost refused to open. The water jets ground to a stop. He looked up at Biton's face, upside down to his own, and smiled.

"Do your arms hurt?"

Starting to shake his head, Cavan switched to a nod. "A little. My shoulders and neck more." Cavan grasped the sides of the tub and stood.

As he stepped out of the water, Biton wrapped him in a large soft towel. "I'll rub some oil on you. It'll help."

Cavan stumbled toward the bedroom with Biton's arm steadying him. So tired… The day was full of ups and downs. None of it mattered now. Biton loved him, wanted him here. Dr. Merten could fuck off.

The thought woke him from his half-asleep state. Even in his mind, he never disrespected anyone. Part of him expected some kind of punishment for his attitude.

Instead, Biton steered him near the bed. Warm hands rubbed the soft towel all over his skin. As he dried him, Biton stole quick kisses, on his neck, chest, thigh...even his butt.

"Climb on the bed, on your stomach."

His arms trembled when he put his weight on them. Easing himself down on the mattress, he buried his face into the soft pillow. The clean fragrance of laundry detergent mixed with Biton's scent. The aroma relaxed him.

Biton's weight shifted the bed but Cavan couldn't force his head to turn enough to look. Warm liquid drizzled on his back. A trickle slid down his side, tickling his skin. Biton's hand caught the stray oil and smeared it up his ribs.

Strong fingers worked his back, digging into aches and pains Cavan hadn't realized were there. The slow steady kneading was different from the way Biton usually touched him. Not sexual...just caring.

Relaxing into his master's hands, Cavan closed his eyes.

———

Biton watched his sleeping lover as the sun crept into the bedroom. Last night had been a breakthrough in his book. Maybe not in Dr. Merten's terms but then he hadn't figured out what she would consider a step forward. He'd talk with her on Monday and find out though.

The sweet oil he'd used to massage Cavan's arms

and back scented the sheets. He'd give him another rub down when he woke up. And maybe some more time in the whirlpool. He'd probably be stiff for a few days.

If they were going to spend more time in the dungeon, and Biton wanted to, Cavan needed to start strengthening his muscles.

Sometime today, they needed to continue their conversation from last night. After a bath and a massage, Cavan had promptly passed out.

Biton also had to break the news about Wainwright's deal with the DA. If he had mixed feelings about the situation, how would Cavan feel?

Climbing out of bed, careful not to wake his lover, Biton grabbed his robe and headed for the kitchen. The leftover Chinese food never made it to the refrigerator. He put on the coffee first then cleared the counter, tossing everything into the trash. Washing the few dishes, he put them away.

After he settled into his recliner with a hot cup of coffee, Biton let his mind concentrate on the discussion last night. Dr. Merten had a lot of explaining to do. Whenever he'd ask about Cavan's therapy, she'd refuse to talk, claiming doctor-patient confidentiality. He'd have to ask her with Cavan there. He'd clear his schedule on Monday so he could take Cavan to his appointment.

The downstairs doorbell buzzed, pulling him from his thoughts. A glance at the clock showed a little after eight. Who would show up here so early on a Saturday?

He flipped the footrest down then rushed to the door. He didn't want Cavan disturbed. He needed to rest.

"Who is it?"

"It's me, Antonio. We need to talk." Antonio's voice, even through the scratchy intercom, didn't sound happy.

"Come on up." Biton pressed the button to release the security doors downstairs. A sense of foreboding swept away the optimism from last night. He waited by the door for Antonio's arrival.

———

Cavan woke alone in the bed. The memory of a noise echoed in his ears. A dream? The front doorbell buzzed. Someone was here?

Climbing out of the wide bed, he grabbed his robe from the footboard. The ache of his shoulders reminded him of last night's pleasure. The sweet smell of the oils Biton rubbed into his muscles swirled in the air as he flipped his robe around him. Voices drifted through the partially open bedroom door.

"We've got a problem," Antonio announced. "Where's Cavan?"

Cavan hesitated at the sound of Mr. Casala's grim voice.

"He's still asleep. What's wrong?" The front door clicked shut.

Eavesdropping didn't feel right. He reached for the doorknob.

"Good. He doesn't need to hear this."

Cavan held his breath. His hand stopped within

inches of the door.

"Come on in the kitchen," Biton said.

Footsteps walked away from Cavan's hidden position. He'd have trouble hearing the conversation with the two men so far away.

If he did it just right…

He opened the door a few more inches, just enough to slip through, then pulled it back the way he'd found it. Staying near the wall, he tiptoed toward the kitchen at an angle. Unless one of the men stood in the doorway, he wouldn't be seen.

"…disappeared last night." Cavan missed the beginning of Antonio's words.

"How? I thought they were being watched."

"Neither of them was under arrest. The department set them up in a halfway house until they could find their families. Only the youngest of the three was put in foster care. Joshua Langley, the one Wainwright called Samuel, is the only one besides Cavan who witnessed Mateo's death."

"I thought he'd refused to testify." Biton's voice was low with an undercurrent of anger.

"He had at the time but I think he was reconsidering. I visited both boys several times, just to keep an eye on them, help them out. They were seeing a therapist, maybe he was ready to talk."

"Do you think Wainwright had something to do with his disappearance?" Biton asked.

"I don't know—either him or the people he's agreed to turn on. If there are no witnesses, then he'll probably walk. You know a jury will misunderstand the BDSM scene. The defense will parade a series of witnesses through talking about the willingness of submissives to accept torture. It would all be played as an accident of brutal lifestyle."

"What about the deal with the DA's office?"

"Yeah, well, if the slave ring's leaders found out about that, they may be the one responsible for Langley's disappearing act." Antonio paused for a few seconds. "How did Cavan take the news about the deal?"

Deal?

Someone exhaled a long sigh. Cavan thought it was Biton.

"I haven't told him yet. After his scare yesterday…"

"What was up with that?" Antonio interrupted.

"Dr. Merton has been pushing him to be more independent. I'm not sure of all the details. He and I need to talk some more."

"Keep him close. I can't post a unit here until I have more proof of a conspiracy or a crime."

Cavan's mind whirled trying to digest the two men's conversation. Could his former master hurt Samuel from jail? And what deal? Lost in his thoughts, he missed the sound of approaching footsteps.

"Cavan!"

He looked up to see Biton in the doorway. "Master…"

"How much did you hear?" Instead of angry, Biton looked almost relieved.

"Most of it but I don't understand."

Biton walked toward him and slipped an arm around his waist. "I'll explain it in a little bit." After a gentle hug, he released him. "Go get dressed while I see Antonio out."

Cavan turned to obey. Biton's hand caught his butt with a quick swat.

"No more eavesdropping."

Darting for the bathroom, he heard the two men talking. This time, he did as he was told and didn't stop to listen.

Chapter Five

Showered, shaved and dressed, Cavan sat at the dining room table toying with his eggs. "So what's the deal Mr. Casala mentioned?" He wasn't sure he wanted more details on Samuel. All the talk about his fellow slaves brought back too many painful memories.

Biton drew a deep breath then pushed away his plate. "The district attorney, the man responsible for prosecuting criminals like your former master, has accepted a deal with Wainwright." He tapped his fingers on the polished wooden table. "Sometimes, criminals have information that can help arrest and convict others who deserve it as much and sometimes more. To get to those people, the DA will make a deal for a lesser charge or a shortened sentence."

"And Mas… my old master has information he wants." Cavan didn't realize he'd clenched his fists until Biton's warm hand covered his.

"Yes. The DA wants the people who sold you and other kids to Wainwright and people like him."

Cavan's mind raced through the concept. "But that's a good thing, right? Making them stop."

"It is but it means Wainwright wouldn't spend as much time in jail. Maybe very little."

"But he killed someone." Cavan glanced up at Biton. "You said he wasn't allowed to do that, even to his slaves."

"He's not but you have to think of how many other children have lived through the same hell you did. How many more could be headed toward a life like that right now." Biton's hand squeezed his. "If the information Wainwright has can stop that, isn't it better he serves less time?"

"I guess." Cavan didn't like the idea of his former master out of jail, able to claim him again.

"This also means you won't have to testify in court. In order for the district attorney to accept the deal, he'll have to plead guilty so there won't be a trial."

A wave of relief swept through Cavan so strong it captured his breath. "No court…" His nightmares of facing the man who nearly killed him, who made him watch while he beat someone to death. The man who forced him to bury a body… "No court…"

When his eyes refocused, his master was kneeling next to Cavan's chair. Strong arms wrapped around him. "No, you'll never have to see him again."

"Good." The word was just a whisper. "Good." This time, he found his voice. "I didn't want to."

"I know you didn't but the fact you were willing means a lot."

"What about Samuel?" None of the slaves under Wainwright's rule talked to each other. It wasn't allowed. He couldn't claim friendship or anything but concern for him worried Cavan.

"Antonio said he disappeared from where he was living. He doesn't know why but, just in case, he wants us to be careful. I don't want you going anywhere without me. That includes Dr. Merten's office."

Cavan's mind returned to their conversation the night before, about telling the truth. "I don't want to go back to Dr. Merten."

"You still have a lot of things to work through." Biton caressed the side of Cavan's face.

"I know." He met Biton's concerned gaze. "But she doesn't want me here with you and I don't want to leave."

"You don't have to leave, no matter what she says. That's a decision only you can make."

"Or you…" Cavan looked down. He was afraid of what he might see.

"I don't want you to leave."

"You never wrote a new contract." His voice wavered on the last word. Questioning his master's desires made him falter.

Biton chuckled. "Is that what's been bothering you lately?"

Keeping his head down, Cavan nodded. "And Dr. Merten."

Rising from his kneeling position, Biton grabbed his chair and scooted it over to face Cavan. "Not all people use written contracts, Cavan. I normally don't. I did the first time with you because you needed something to hang on to. I thought it would make it easier for you to obey me. I needed information. Would you have told me about Mateo if you weren't completely sure I was your master?"

Cavan closed his eyes as memories of that first month with Biton swirled through his mind. The dizzying thoughts kept coming back to one place. "So you didn't want me. You just needed me to talk."

"Hey, look at me." Fingers tapped Cavan's cheek.

Cavan's gaze met his master's dark eyes.

"I was interested in you. That's why I invited you to lunch. Remember? I needed you to talk, that's why I offered the contract. But you're still here because I love you and I want you to stay." Biton leaned forward and brushed his lips against Cavan's. "If you want a contract, I'll write one but trusting each other is more important than words on paper."

Leaning into the warmth of Biton's breath, Cavan sought his master's mouth. Sweet nipping kisses turned hungry. His hands grasped at Biton's shoulders. "I love you," he murmured between breaths.

Biton wrapped him in a strong embrace. He pulled him to his feet, setting plates rattling when Cavan's body bumped the table. Strong hands shoved under Cavan's t-shirt, heating his skin. The soft material bunched up under his arms. His master's body pressed against him.

His growing erection ground against Cavan's groin.

His cock responded with enthusiasm. Cavan slipped his hands down the back of Biton's jeans. Grasping the firm flesh, he pulled his master closer. Eager lips covered Cavan's mouth. He welcomed Biton's moist tongue, meeting the thrusting flesh with his own.

One of Biton's hands switched directions and headed south. Slipping past his ass, fingers dug into Cavan's thigh and tugged.

Cavan lifted his leg then crooked his knee around Biton's ass. The change in angle aligned their cocks. Two layers of jeans aided the heated friction. Urgency threw Cavan off balance. Biton's hands tried to steady him but lost his hold. Cavan fell against the table pushing it several inches. His hand slammed down on the polished wood as he caught himself.

The vase in the middle rocked then settled among the rattling china and silverware.

A gurgle of laughter erupted from Biton's throat. "Of all the places better suited to sex, we have to try it standing up against the dining room table." Biton tugged him upright.

"Don't care." Cavan adjusted his footing while he pushed Biton's shirt up. Flat dark nipples peeked out of the broad, fur covered chest. Before Biton could say another word, Cavan's tongue circled a tiny morsel of flesh.

Biton's aureole puckered and the nipple perked up. A large hand caught the back of Cavan's head, encouraging him forward.

Cavan's fingers fumbled with the button and zipper of Biton's jeans. The need to give pleasure to his master outweighed place and propriety. His mind, reeling with relief, didn't consider asking permission or waiting for Biton's command. Biton wanted him, loved him.

When the heat of Biton's cock filled his hand, Cavan moaned around the sharp point of Biton's nipple. Fingers dug into Cavan's hair, nails scraping his scalp.

Kissing a path from Biton's chest to his stomach, Cavan dropped to his knees. His hands yanked at the denim partially confining Biton's cock. He peeled away the soft cotton briefs, revealing his master's thick flesh.

The slit in the crown glistened with a tiny drop of moisture. Cavan curled his tongue around the head, circling several times before he reached the center. Teasing the small opening rewarded him with more clear liquid. The slightly bitter taste exploded through his taste buds. His tongue moved on to the sensitive underside, just below the crown.

Mumbled words of encouragement floated above his head. Biton's hands cupped Cavan's head. His fingers teased through his hair.

Sucking the head into his mouth, he continued tormenting the tender spot with his tongue. His fingers pulled the tight jeans past Biton's hips. The black cotton briefs followed next.

Biton's hips flexed, pressing his cock deeper. His hands tightened around the back of Cavan's head.

His first instinct was to let his master take his

pleasure but a perverse kernel of an idea crept into Cavan's mind. *Choice.*

His hands gripped Biton's hips and held tight. Biton's motioned stopped with a surprised grunt.

A quick glance at Biton showed an indulgent smile on his master's face. Cavan pulled back, sucking hard, he released Biton's flesh with a loud pop. Flashing Biton a quick grin, Cavan recaptured the silky head.

Suckling the crown, his teeth caught the edge with a gentle scrape.

Biton's body shuddered and a low moan vibrated through him. His hands fluttered around Cavan's head, petting and caressing but not restricting.

Cavan slipped one hand between Biton's thighs. The wrinkled sac tightened as his fingers teased the skin.

With his jeans restricting Biton's legs, Cavan couldn't quite get the angle right. He let go of the heated flesh with a sigh. Pushing Biton toward the chair he'd recently occupied, Cavan scooted along on his knees. Biton took the hint and sat.

Anxious with the need to give his master pleasure, Cavan slid Biton's jeans and underwear down his long legs and past his bare feet.

Biton opened his legs wide and slumped down in the chair until his ass hung off the edge. His dark eyes watched, half-lidded with lust, as Cavan crawled forward.

Instead of returning to the leaking cock, Cavan dove between the muscular thighs. His tongue bathed

Biton's balls like a cat cleaning its fur.

"Feels good…" Biton moaned. His fingers curled into fists and rested on his thighs. His body arched slightly toward Cavan's hungry mouth.

Cavan shouldered Biton's leg up on his back. With better access, he sucked one of the spongy balls into his mouth. His tongue alternated between prodding and laving.

Biton reached for his cock then began stroking while Cavan moved to the other ball. Panting breath paused for a soft groan. "Yeah…"

Parting his master's ass cheeks, Cavan pressed in toward a new target. The tiny puckered hole clenched as his tongue prodded against it. The angle was awkward. His neck and jaw ached but Biton's moan of pleasure kept him from moving away. Instead, he tugged at Biton's hips until he scooted farther down in the chair.

His lower back on the cushioned seat, Biton's hands reached behind his head and grasped the slatted chair back.

With better access, Cavan laved the tight hole. The ring of nerves quivered with each pass. Rolling his tongue into a point, he pushed into the puckered flesh. The muscles relaxed to accept him.

Using the tip of one finger, Cavan tugged at the edge of Biton's hole. The action opened him enough that Cavan's tongue went deeper.

Biton's whole body jerked. Cavan's finger slipped inside, almost to the first knuckle.

"Yes." Biton groaned. "Push it in."

Cavan pulled away, both tongue and finger. "Master?"

"Your finger. Push it in." Biton fisted his cock. The angry red tip gleamed with pre-cum.

Confusion made Cavan hesitate. He'd never penetrated his master with anything more than his tongue. Even then, not as deep as he'd done today.

"It's okay." Biton's gaze met his. "Just do it." His dark eyes glowed with desire.

Nodding more to himself than his master, Cavan circled his finger around the puckered ring gathering saliva. A gentle push against Biton's hole and his finger slid in again. This time, he didn't stop until the second knuckle disappeared into the tight heat.

Biton's hand pulled his cock with long fast strokes. His eyes rolled back before his eyelids hid them from view. "Yes. Curl your finger up."

Understanding what his master wanted, Cavan turned his hand so his finger could seek out the hard knot of Biton's prostate.

Biton's ass clenched around Cavan's hand. His body shook with pleasure. "Fuck." His hand lost its rhythm. "Fuck, yes!"

Without stopping to ask permission, Cavan straightened and leaned over Biton's weeping flesh. His free hand pulled Biton's away from his engorged cock. He took Biton's full length in one long swallow. With his fingers gripping the base, he fucked his mouth with his master's dick, hard and fast.

He matched the pace with his finger, stroking the

tight ass, poking the sensitive gland each time.

Biton's arm muscles bulged as he held on to the chair. His taut body rocked with tiny movements but let Cavan take the lead.

His hands occupied, Cavan's cock protested the lack of contact with anything other than his tight jeans. His hips jerked as he sought some kind of relief.

Biton's leg shifted below him. Seizing the opportunity, Cavan rubbed his groin against Biton's calf.

With a strangled cry, Biton let go. His cock spurted thick hot fluid down Cavan's throat. His ass muscles clenched like a vice around Cavan's finger. Pushing against Biton's grip, Cavan pressed against his prostate and held tight against the hard knot.

Another guttural moan and gasping breaths accompanied another jolt of cum. Cavan didn't stop. His mouth worked the jerking length, forcing the last of Biton's seed into his mouth.

"Fuck!" Biton's hands scrabbled for Cavan's head and yanked him away. The loss of his grip on the back of the chair sent his body sliding to the floor. Cavan's hand pulled free of Biton's ass. With legs sprawled on either side of Cavan, Biton grabbed Cavan by the hair.

Hard, greedy kisses covered Cavan's mouth. Almost numb lips fumbled to return Biton's enthusiasm. His aching cock throbbed for relief. He tugged at the button on his jeans only to have his hands knocked away by Biton's.

Before he could mourn the loss of Biton's lips, Cavan

found himself sprawled back on the hard wooden floor. Biton ripped open his jeans and yanked them down his hips. As his master's mouth closed on his cock, Cavan's body convulsed in ecstasy. The muscles in his lower stomach tensed to the point of cramping as he emptied into Biton's mouth.

Cavan's body jerked with aftershocks. Biton kissed his way up Cavan's body through his sweat damp t-shirt. His heavy weight settled on Cavan.

"Damn." Biton nipped at Cavan's panting mouth. "That was good."

Cavan closed his eyes with relief. He didn't understand what had come over him. Pushing his master around, ignoring his silent clues. Biton liked what he'd done in spite of the implied disobedience. Was this what Biton meant by a relationship?

———

Biton kept a close eye on Cavan for the rest of the morning. He was quiet but not really withdrawn. He wondered what was going on his lover's mind.

Seated at the dining room table, Biton reviewed some notes for a deposition next week. Cavan, opposite him, had his cookbooks out and a piece of paper and pencil writing his shopping list.

Biton kept his smile hidden. Cavan's painstaking scrawl from a few months ago had smoothed out. He jotted down ingredients as if he'd been writing all his life. His reading had increased as well. He went through more books each week. Although Biton could more than afford to buy him all the books he wanted, he didn't have the space to store them. Today, he'd introduce Cavan to the public library. There was a branch a few blocks from the apartment. It would add to the things Cavan could learn to do on his own.

A frown interrupted his thoughts. With Antonio's warning, it wouldn't be wise to have Cavan out alone. For now, he'd make sure he went with him.

"What's wrong?"

Biton glance across the table. "I was just thinking about what Antonio said—about Samuel."

"Do you think he's okay?"

"I don't know." Biton set his pen down. "How well did you know Samuel?"

Cavan never spoke much about his relationship with the other slaves. Biton wondered if he talked about them to Dr. Merten.

"As well as any of the others." Cavan shrugged. "Wainwright didn't like us to talk." His gaze dropped to the pad in front of him. "We…we had sex sometimes." His hand curled into a tight fist. "Wainwright liked to watch."

"You don't have to talk about it if you don't want to." Biton reached across the table and caressed Cavan's hand.

"It's okay." He opened his hand and turned it palm up. Grasping Biton's hand, he brought it up to his lips. Gentle kisses trailed across Biton's knuckles. "Dr. Merten is always trying to make me talk about them."

"And you don't?"

"She wouldn't understand."

"Why not?" Biton squeezed Cavan's hand.

"I…I didn't want to do the things my master demanded. When he chose another slave, I was always…relieved." Cavan hesitated but Biton stayed silent. His head lowered until Biton could see only the top of his head. "Is it wrong to wish that on someone else?"

"In a way, yes."

Cavan's head jerked up. A surprised look mixed with anguish.

"But your wishes didn't change anything. Wainwright did what he wanted because he was a cruel man, not because of anything you thought. Nothing that happened to you or any of the other men in his house was your fault or your choice."

"I didn't want him to hurt them. I just didn't want him to hurt me either." Sadness lowered his eyelids.

"I know." Biton let go of Cavan's hand then shut the folder in front of him. "I have an idea. Let's go to the library before we go shopping."

"The library?"

"Yes. Did you ever go to one as a kid?" Biton pushed his chair back and stood.

Cavan tore the top piece of paper from his notepad. "I think so. Lots of books that you didn't have to buy."

"Yep. You just borrow them for a couple of weeks or so and then bring them back once you've read them."

Light returned to Cavan's pale green eyes. Nothing like the prospect of a new book to distract him.

Cavan stared at his shopping list as Biton drove the car out of the apartment building's underground garage.

"The library is only a few blocks away. We'll go shopping from there."

Nodding Cavan looked up. The narrow one-way street was quiet. The neighborhood was set off the main streets. Sometimes Cavan felt like he was going from one town to another just leaving their block.

Biton stopped behind a van waiting at the stop sign. "After everything is settled with Wainwright, you'll be able to walk to the library on your own whenever you want."

Another car pulled up behind them. Through the side mirror, Cavan saw a man climb out of the passenger side. His arm crooked behind him as if he were hiding something.

"Biton." The man walked toward the car in a hurry. "That man…"

A crowbar slammed Cavan's window. Shattered glass flew through the car. Stinging shards spattered Cavan's face and arms.

"Cavan!" Biton reached for him.

A sharp pain lanced through Cavan's head. Darkness engulfed him as a gunshot rang out. The acrid smell of gunpowder followed him into oblivion.

Chapter Six

The rancid odor of human waste and something worse assaulted Cavan's nostrils. His head throbbed in rapid pace with his heartbeat.

Something was wrong.

His eyes opened but the room was too dark to see more than shadows. Cold concrete beneath him and the lack of light confirmed he wasn't home. It was as if time had rewound. He was in a cell like the one where he'd spent nine years of his life.

Where was Biton? Or was it just a dream and this nightmare was reality?

Panic clutched his throat and interfered with his breathing. Gasping for air, he tried to filter through his memories, figure out what happened.

"Calm," he whispered between breaths. "Calm."

Lying still on the floor, he searched for the last thing he remembered.

"Biton. Dining room." The picture was almost there. "Sucking him." The image flooded his memory. Sex in the dining room.

"After that?" His fingers curled as if holding a pencil. "Shopping list." He dragged himself to a sitting position. His head punished him for the effort with sharp lancing pain. "My shopping list." He dug into his pockets for the piece of paper but found nothing. "How will I know what to buy?"

A short snort of laughter escaped. He wouldn't be shopping today.

Where was Biton? Something nagged his memory—something not good—but it wouldn't surface.

Antonio's visit. He said Samuel disappeared and for Cavan to be careful.

"Samuel?" Using the wall behind him, Cavan inched his way to his feet. The painful throbbing in his head got worse the higher he got.

He reached up to touch the place that ached the most. Sticky with something…blood. The copper smell brought back the memory of his former master, of the whip eating away his flesh, blood flowing down his back.

With his hand on the wall to steady him, he shuffled toward the crack of light that indicated an opening. Feeling his way across the cold metal door, he searched for a doorknob but there wasn't one. His fingers traced the keyhole on what was probably a deadbolt locked from the outside.

Dizziness forced him back to the floor. Nausea

roiled through his stomach. Where was Biton? Darkness settled on him again.

———

Biton grimaced against the pain lancing his shoulder. The nurse's hands were sure but gentle didn't seem to factor into her job duties.

The bandage tightened across his chest and up over his wounded shoulder. "I'm done now, Mr. Savakis. Lay back and relax. I'll bring you some pain medication."

"I'm not staying here." He swung his legs off the exam table. "I need to talk to the police right now."

"A Detective Casala is outside waiting to speak to you." She pushed his legs back up on the bed. "Lay back."

Biton leaned against the elevated head of the bed. He'd wait until she left.

Her eyebrow arched at him. Maybe mind reading was part of her repertoire. She turned and disappeared through the curtains surrounding the exam table.

Antonio burst through before the material stopped swinging. "What the fuck happened?"

"A van and a car blocked me in on the street. A man, tall, sunglasses and a baseball hat, got out of the car behind me and busted the passenger side window with a crowbar. He hit Cavan in the head and pulled him from the car." Biton's throat tightened. "Someone in the van opened the back doors and took a shot at me. They threw Cavan in the van and took off."

"And the one behind you?"

"Backed down into a driveway, turned around and took off."

"Descriptions?"

Biton closed his eyes. "The van was a white cargo van. Windows in the back were tinted. A Dodge. No markings that I could see." The picture of Cavan's limp form being shoved into the vehicle kept replaying behind his eyelids. "The car was a sedan, four doors, dark—black maybe blue. It was dirty, hard to tell the exact color. Looked like a Crown Vic."

"Tags?"

"The ones on the van were Jersey plates but the numbers were coated in dried mud. I couldn't read them. The car… I couldn't focus…" And they took Cavan. "I shouldn't have left the house. I didn't think they'd find him there. Who knew where we live?"

"I don't know. Some of the papers turned over to the defense had your name in there from the original questioning by Detective Ramos. Other than that, nothing was listed about his living arrangements."

"They could have found me. It's not as if my name is common and it's listed on the firm's website. An internet search would have turned up my office but not my home."

"They could have followed you." Antonio made some notes on his pad.

"Do you have any clues yet?"

"None. The DA is questioning Wainwright now. He hadn't given up any names yet. Kept 'renegotiating' the deal."

"Stalling you mean."

"Yeah. I'm afraid that's exactly what he was doing. Waiting for his associates to round up the witnesses." Antonio scrubbed his hand over his face. "We'll put a bulletin out on the vehicles but they were probably stolen."

"I've got to get out of here. I can't just lay here and wait."

Antonio squeezed his uninjured right arm. "You've lost a lot of blood. Passing out in the street won't do Cavan any good."

"Either I go with you or I go alone but I won't stay."

His friend hesitated but then nodded. "I guess I couldn't sit still if I were in your position either."

"I need a shirt."

Antonio picked up the ragged remains of Biton's polo shirt. The nurse had cut it off him to tend the wound. Even without the shredding, the material was soaked in blood.

"I'll find you something." He disappeared through the curtains.

Biton lay back with a sigh of relief. The blood loss had taken its toll. His body trembled from a chill he knew was shock. He refused to give in. He had to find Cavan. His lover trusted him to keep him safe. No telling what nightmare from his past he was reliving.

The hope that Cavan was still alive refused to give up also. If they'd just wanted him dead, he would have been left in the car with a bullet to the head. Whoever had him, wanted information. Biton prayed

SHAYLA KERSTEN

to whatever deities might be listening that Cavan kept his head about him. They needed time to find him.

Footsteps, too soft for Antonio, approached the exam area. The nurse slipped between the curtains. She offered a small paper container with two pills. Her other hand held a cup of water.

"What are they?"

"Pain pills. OxyContin to be exact."

"No thanks. I need to be awake." He crossed his good arm over the injured one. "I'm leaving."

"You are in no shape to be larking off. The police will have more questions. You can't help your friend if you go into shock somewhere." She glared over the top of her glasses.

"I'm leaving with the police so you don't have to worry about me."

Antonio picked the perfect time for an entrance. He tossed a bag from the hospital gift shop on the bed.

The nurse transfixed her fierce look on Antonio. "What is that?"

Biton emptied the bag. A dark blue t-shirt flopped out. "Help me put it on."

Antonio wavered under the nurse's stare but moved to Biton's side. "It's all they had. I got it extra large so maybe it won't be too bad getting your arm through." He shook the folded shirt out. A skyline of New York was emblazoned across the front.

"Just get it on me."

The nurse gave up and left, carrying the meds and water with her.

FOREVER

Cavan woke to noise outside his cell. The nightmare hadn't ended. Muffed moans and slamming doors, footsteps coming closer. A key scraped the lock to his door. The click echoed in Cavan's mind. His heart raced while he waited for the door to open.

Part of him hoped Biton would be on the other side, ready to take him home, but reality said his dream wouldn't happen.

Light flooded the dim cell, blinding him for a few seconds. It was enough time for his captor to get to him and blindfold him. Rough hands pulled him to his feet. Ropes cut his wrists as the man bound his arms behind him. Keys jangled against something solid then stilled.

"Move." A sharp jab in his back prodded Cavan forward.

Nine years of instincts took over. He'd worked so hard to become the man Biton wanted him to be. Now, all he could do was obey.

Shuffling forward, he let his captor guide him toward the unknown. Or maybe back into a hell he'd known all too well.

The memory of Biton's gentle hands seemed distant—a dream instead of his life for the last four months.

He stumbled on something. Without his arms to steady him, he fell to the hard floor. His captor kicked his thigh barely missing his groin.

"Get the fuck up."

Cavan twisted his legs under him in a kneeling position, his toes curled under him. Rocking backward, he rolled to his feet.

A hard slap across the face rewarded his obedience.

Anger surged through him. He bit his lip, forcing back a question; the only question he wanted to ask right now. Why?

With a push from the man behind him, Cavan started forward again.

"Stop."

With one foot still in the air, Cavan stood perfectly still. The muscles in his arms, still tender from hanging in the playroom last night, trembled with the tightly bound ropes.

"Step up."

Cavan rocked his foot forward and encountered something solid. He found the top of the stair and planted his foot on it. Raising his other leg, his left foot joined his right. He kept a slow pace up the stairs until the last one.

Twelve. There were twelve steps.

Not Master Wainwright's house. He had fifteen steps. His relief was short lived. He was still a captive with an unknown jailer.

Another person stood in front of him. Hot breath, foul and almost as rank as the cell, blew across his face. Rough leather circled his neck. A collar. Someone was claiming him. Only Biton could claim him that way.

"No!" The word sounded like his voice but he couldn't believe he said it.

This time the hand that hit him wasn't open. A hard fist met his lips. Blood tasted sharp in his mouth.

"I'll do whatever I want to you. You are nothing but a fucking slave. I'll collar you and use you like the slut you are."

Another blow, this time to his stomach, took away his breath. A third hit sent him to his knees.

A large hand grabbed his hair from behind and yanked his head up. The man in front of him growled close to his face. "And if you don't please me. I'll make what Wainwright did to you look like a picnic."

Whips, blood, pain… Cavan's instinct sent the only words it could to his bleeding mouth. "Yes, Master."

———

Sitting back in Antonio's car, Biton gasped for air. Sweat streamed down his face and torso. The t-shirt was already soaked.

Maybe he should have negotiated with the nurse for something less debilitating than OxyContin. His shoulder throbbed with intense pain. The bullet had gone completely through. He had muscle damage but nothing that wouldn't heal with some physical therapy. No major arteries or veins were hit. Knowing the damage was minimal didn't make it less painful.

The knowledge of what Cavan could be going through got air back in his lungs.

"You okay?" Antonio put the key in the ignition. "We can go back in." Turning on the car, he pushed the air conditioner up to high and pointed the vents

Biton's direction. "You *do* realize you look like shit."

"Just go. Get to the precinct and see if there's any word." Biton groaned as he tried to pull the seatbelt around him.

Antonio leaned over and fastened it for him. "Yeah, and Lia's going to have my ass in a sling for a change when she finds out I sprung you from the ER."

"You might like it," Biton growled. He closed his eyes against the dizzying traffic passing by.

"They wanted him alive, Biton. Keep thinking about that."

"I am. I have to believe he's alive and I'll get him back." Biton's throat tightened. "I promised to keep him safe."

"This isn't your fault. Who would expect an attack in broad daylight, in an upper class neighborhood?"

"You said to be careful. We should have stayed in." Biton shook his head. "We've become predictable. If they were watching, they'd have known we always go out on Saturday. I wanted to create stability for Cavan. Routines help."

"There's no way to know how long someone has been watching. They could've just seized an opportunity."

Biton didn't want logical explanations. "Do you think the DA will get Wainwright to talk?"

"In light of what's happened… I don't know. I think he was stringing us along waiting for this to happen. The DA still thinks he's on the up and up."

"Give me five minutes alone with him."

Antonio barked a laugh. "In your condition? He'd

push you over with a finger."

As much as he wanted to object, Biton couldn't. Nausea turned his stomach into knots. He wouldn't be much help but he couldn't sit in a hospital and wait for news. He made up his mind to be as little hindrance as possible.

The car rolled to a stop and the engine kicked off.

Biton opened his eyes to see the precinct. Now to make it in the building without passing out.

———

Cavan knelt in the same position for what seemed an eternity. His arms had been unbound with orders for him not to move. The blindfold firmly in place, he listened for anyone around him. The collar chafed in more ways than physical.

In his old life, he could remain motionless for hours without thinking about anything, his mind a complete blank. Now, his thoughts whirled around seeking answers. First—how did he get here and where was Biton?

He knew the two were related. He rarely went anywhere without his master, unless it was to Dr. Merten's office. What day was it? His head ached and his swollen lip throbbed. His stomach would probably bruise from the punch; his thigh, too, from where the first man kicked him.

All his aches and pains didn't hurt as much as not knowing where Biton was. Something nagged his fragmented memory. Every time he pulled a few pieces together, they scattered like pigeons on the avenue.

Footsteps approached then circled him. Fingers teased his hair in a gentle caress. The silence of his tormentor was unnerving. He tensed in anticipation of the next blow.

"Your hair is too long, slave." A sharp tug caught Cavan off guard. "Your master always required clean shaven slaves."

Cavan opened his mouth to answer but stopped. The man would give permission if he wanted Cavan to speak.

"It looks like you need a refresher course in your training." He continued around before stopping in front of Cavan. His hand caught Cavan's face and pinched.

The thumb digging into the left side of his mouth aggravated his swollen lip. A gasp of pain escaped.

"That's just what I mean. You weren't supposed to make *any* noise." His hand wrenched Cavan's jaw before he released him. "I guess I'll have to remind you of proper training."

Cavan bit his lip to keep from moaning. Fresh blood leaked into his mouth. Fear warred with stronger feelings lurking deep.

A drawer opened and closed. "I guess Biton Savakis wasn't much of a dominant. He let your training go to hell." The snap of a whip sent a shudder through Cavan. "Well, we don't have to worry about him any more. You're back with the right kind of people. And you will obey me. Or I'll finish what Wainwright failed to do."

Footsteps circled him, more than one set. "Put him on the cross. Tie him tight."

A knock at the door stopped both men. "I said I wasn't to be disturbed." The master's harsh voice made Cavan wince.

"I'm sorry, sir. Phone call. Tanner said it's urgent," a third voice said.

"Damn." The man's footsteps retreated then the door clicked shut.

Three. At least three people holding him here. He should just shut down his mind, try to block the pain with nothingness. The whipping would hurt less and go faster if he didn't react too much.

Whipping. Panic rose up and clutched his throat. He had to get out of here.

Calm down. You can't think if you freak out. His internal voice of reason, something he'd started to recognize, made sense. He forced his breathing slower. His ears strained for any sound.

Nothing. No movement, not even another person breathing. They must have all left.

Cavan slowly raised his hands. No one yelled at him for moving. He yanked the blindfold free. The buckle of the collar followed. The dungeon wasn't familiar. Not some place Wainwright had taken him before. His former master rarely took his slaves out but on occasion, he'd supply one for a party.

No phone, one exit, no closets he could hide in. No way out but the same door the others had used.

A long single tail whip lay on a table. A St. Andrew's cross stood in the middle of the room.

A shudder racked Cavan's spine. He wouldn't let them whip him. Not again.

He tiptoed to the door, thankful they hadn't taken his clothes yet, only his shoes. His breath stopped as he turned the doorknob. No sound on the other side. Yet. Pulling the heavy wooden door open, he listened for sounds.

The master's angry voice echoed down the hall from the right. "I don't care what he wants. Until I find out what he and the other one have said, tell your client to keep his fucking mouth shut."

Cavan didn't waste time. He slipped out the door and turned left. His sense of direction, unless he was turned around, told him this was the way he came. He only hoped there was a way out and not just a return to the basement cell.

He scampered down the hall to the end, past open doors—a living room, a bedroom, another room full of books. Two doors at the end of the hall were closed. He grabbed the doorknob of the first one. Stairs led into darkness. The dank smell told him he'd found the basement where he'd been held. He started to close the door when a soft moan floated up from below.

"The other one…" That's what the master had said. "Samuel." Cavan breathed his name.

Fear urged him out of the house but a spark of conscience made him hesitate. He couldn't leave Samuel. The master would be very angry. Cavan would be leaving Samuel to take his place.

But if Cavan could get free, get to a phone, he could call for help.

The master's shouting sounded through the hall. "That cowardly son of a bitch. If he starts talking, he'll ruin everything. I told his sniveling lawyer I'd deal with this."

Cavan ducked into the stairwell of the dungeon and pulled the door nearly closed. He listened as footsteps stormed down the hall.

"Get the other one up here now. I'll beat it out of both of them."

There was nowhere to run. If the man came to the basement he'd find Cavan.

"Son of a bitch! Find Cavan. He got away."

The yell sent Cavan barreling down the stairs into the darkness.

Chapter Seven

Biton watched Wainwright through the one-way glass. His attorney had asked for a few moments alone with his client. The law required the police to shut off the intercom. Antonio followed procedure then he glanced at Biton.

"I need to use the john." He turned and hurried out of the room, leaving Biton alone with deliberate temptation.

Slamming the intercom button, Biton eavesdropped on privileged information.

"I'm not going to jail forever to protect his ass. You said this would be over before I had to cough up any names." Wainwright's anger mingled with fear. "Do you know what they'll do to me inside the pen? These fucking cops will spread the rumor that I molested children. I'll be dead in a month."

A smile curved Biton's lips. The man was right.

Even the most hardened killers wouldn't stand for a sexual predator in their midst.

"You just have to hang on for another few hours. He has to find out what they told the cops. You know he can get it out of them."

"No, I don't have to do anything. You get him on the phone, right now, and tell him the game is over. Dispose of those two and I walk. He doesn't have time to play games. If they'd given up his name, he'd already be in here with me."

The attorney, James Tanner, shook his head. "It's too dangerous to call him. The call could be traced."

"Yeah, and I can make sure he shares the same fate. Call him."

Biton clenched his fists. His heart skipped a beat at the word 'dispose'. "Yes, you idiot, Tanner. Call him."

The door rattled behind Biton. He punched the intercom off as the door opened. Biton's eyes never left Tanner. The man pulled out a cell phone and dialed.

"Trace that call."

"What?" Antonio stepped up beside him. Assistant District Attorney Luca settled on the other side.

"Trace that call. They were arguing over something and then Tanner pulled out his phone. He doesn't look happy about it." Biton turned to Antonio. "Please just trace the call."

Antonio glanced over Biton's shoulder. "Okay." He pulled out his phone as he walked out of the viewing room.

"You didn't do anything to get our case into trouble,

did you?"

"No," Biton lied. "I just think that if it's important enough for Tanner to be calling someone in the middle of Wainwright's deal negotiations, it's important for us to know who he called."

"Attorney-client privilege applies to phone calls."

"Yes, it does. But only to the conversation. I just want to know who he's calling."

Luca nodded. "Agreed."

Turning back to the window, he watched Tanner's back as his hand gestured wildly. "He's not happy."

"No. And something tells me he's going to be even less so," Luca agreed.

The door flipped open. "The trace is in to the cell phone company." Antonio walked up behind Biton. "We'll know in a few minutes."

"Luca?" Biton kept his voice soft.

"Yes?"

"This time. No deals."

"No deals," Luca agreed.

Cavan heard footsteps rush past the door above him. He needed to find the key to Samuel's cell. Even if there were no way out of the basement, two of them would have a better chance against three.

Shock made him pause. He planned to fight a master. "Yes, damn it. I'm not going to do what he wants. It's my choice." His mind chanted the words like a calming prayer...*my choice.*

His hands flitted along the walls looking for keys. When he was taken from his cell, it sounded like the keys were left here. He didn't want to turn on the light. The last place he thought they'd look for him would be the basement. Light showing under the door would give him away.

A sharp object bit into his finger. The jangle of keys greeted him.

"Yes..." he whispered. He snagged them off the hook. Now to find Samuel.

Earlier, the sound of the other person seemed to come from the left of Cavan's cell but he had no idea which one he'd been imprisoned in.

"Samuel?" The hoarse whisper sounded loud. His heartbeat sounded louder. No sign of movement from the floor above. "Samuel, where are you?"

"Who's there?" The weak voice came from his right.

"It's Cavan. I'm going to get you out. Keep talking so I can find you."

"We're not supposed to talk." Samuel's words were almost a whine. "They'll beat me again."

"Not if we can get out of here." He followed the words to the end of the row of cells. High up in the wall, a few flecks of sunlight shone through. A window—covered with black paint. He fitted the key to the lock. "Come on." Pushing the door open, the smell of blood and vomit almost overwhelmed him. He choked back bile threatening to rise. His eyes adjusted to the dim light from the window. A lump in the middle of the floor moved.

"How do we get out?" The whimpering man started to stand but his legs couldn't seem to hold him.

"You have to walk. I don't care how much it hurts. I can't carry you. And there's no way I can get you out that window," he pointed up, "without your help."

"I can't…"

Cavan's anger boiled toward a breaking point. He wasn't someone's toy to be used and traded. Neither was Samuel. These men had no right to do the things they did. "Yes, you can. Now shut the fuck up and stand."

Samuel obeyed without another word. He shuffled through the door and into the thin rays of light. His jeans were ragged but intact. No shirt. Dark stains striped his ribs. The whip must have wrapped his body.

He needed something to break the window. Nothing along the walls but the keys. "Can you lift me?" Cavan stripped his shirt over his head and wrapped his hand and wrist in it.

"I don't think so."

"I only need to go up a foot. I have to break the window."

Samuel looked up for the first time since he came out of his cell. A sparkle of life lit his eye when the sunlight hit it. "I love the sunlight. So many years in the dark."

"Me too. But we have to get out of here to see it." Cavan unwrapped his hand. "Here. Hold out your hand." He covered Samuel's hand in the soft cotton. "I'm going to give you a lift up. Break out the glass and clear as much away from the frame as you can."

244

"Okay." His hand shook under Cavan's.

"You can do it. Then we'll be in the sunshine and away from here." He released Samuel and bent over. Leaning against the wall for support, he cupped his hands together. He glanced at Samuel. "Now."

An unsteady step and Samuel was eye level with the small window. He hesitated for a second then punched the window with a weak blow. The glass cracked but didn't shatter.

"Again," Cavan urged. Aching muscles protested the other man's weight.

Another hit and glass rained down on Cavan. He closed his eyes as sunlight streamed into the room.

"Clear the glass from the frame."

Tinkling of fragments fell both inside and out of the building. The sound of the door above pushed Cavan into motion. "Go, Samuel. Get out. Get help!" Puffing with exertion, he shoved Samuel upward.

Fear must have put strength in Samuel's arms. He pulled himself through the tiny space.

Cavan didn't look at the men racing for him. Instead, he leaped for the window ledge. Bits of glass cut into his hands as his toes scrabbled for a foothold to boost him up.

"Not so fucking fast." Hands grabbed his legs, then his waist and pulled.

"No! No! No!"

———

Biton drummed his fingers along his thigh. The

police car sped through the streets with lights and sirens but it couldn't go fast enough for Biton.

"It may be a false alarm." Antonio tried to be the voice of reason.

Of course, he didn't know what Biton heard in the interrogation room. And he could never know. No one could. Antonio's career would be over for leaving Biton alone when Tanner requested privacy.

"I know. But it's all we've got."

"I've never heard of Simon Fairfield. He's not part of the scene. Or at least anyone I've heard of." Antonio made a sharp right down the avenue.

The turn combined with pressure from the seatbelt sent a burning stab of pain lancing through Biton's shoulder. "Even if he's trafficking in sex slaves, he may not be into using them. He might just be in it for the money."

"Maybe." Antonio glanced at Biton. "You know when we get there, you can't come in with us."

"I know."

"Don't placate me. You have to stay outside."

"I will. I promise." Biton clenched his fist. "I need to be there…just in case."

———

Cavan kicked at the two men trying to force him up the stairs. The master stood at the top of the stairwell holding a whip in his hand and an insane anger in his beady eyes. His tall thin frame shook with fury.

"Samuel got out the window," the taller, bulkier

man yelled.

"Damn it, Karl." The man slapped Karl as they emerged from the basement. "I'll take this one. Go find Samuel." He punched Cavan's already bruised mouth.

Pain hampered Cavan's struggle. Karl released his right arm as the master grabbed it. Half dragging Cavan down the hall, he continued yelling. "I'll filet the skin off your back for this. You'll die a death worse than Mateo ever suffered."

Recognition dawned on Cavan. This was the man who upset Wainwright enough to kill.

The master released his arm as the other man dragged Cavan through the door.

Cavan seized the opportunity. Relaxing his body, he fell to the floor. The man holding him lost his grip. Cavan rolled away and to his feet. He couldn't get out the door so he ran toward the cross in the middle of the room and then around it.

The master's whip lashed out. The tail caught Cavan's lower back. The stinging bite tore a gasp from his throat but he didn't slow down.

A quick glance around the room gave him ideas for weapons. The idea of striking a master nearly incapacitated him.

The whip struck again, missing Cavan but catching the side of the cross.

"I'm not your slave. I'm not anyone's slave." Cavan screamed across the room. "I won't let you beat me."

"You don't have a choice. You will die here today."

Cavan darted toward a wall of implements, leaving

the slim cover of the cross. The other man in the room circled around toward him as he ran.

"Samuel went for help. When the police get here, when Biton finds me…"

A harsh laugh ripped through the master. "Your precious master won't be coming for you. He's dead."

"No. Not possible." Cavan's determination faltered. He paused within a foot of his intended weapon.

"Oh, did I forget to mention that?" The man's weasel face crooked up in a smile. "So sorry." He pointed to the other man. "Robert here had to shoot him. He tried to keep us from taking you."

"No…" The memory of gunfire, gunpowder, echoed in Cavan's mind. "He's not dead."

"Oh, but so sad for you, he is." The master kept moving toward Cavan. His whip flicked back as he prepared to strike. "But don't worry, you'll join him soon enough." As the whip lashed out, Robert ran toward Cavan.

Reaching for a thick metal rod, Cavan yanked it from the wall as the whip circled his waist.

The metal crunched bone as he slammed it into Robert's face. The man went down screaming.

Only now, the master's eyes showed a sign of anything other than cruelty. Cavan recognized his new expression. He'd seen his own fear reflected enough in the mirror.

Grabbing the whip with his left hand, he held on. The master circled out of reach of the iron bar, his hand still gripping the single tail's handle.

"Biton was only helping me." Cavan yanked the whip and it jerked free of the weasel's hand. Still holding the bar, he pulled the whip toward him. "He loved me. Wanted me for me. Not as a toy to abuse." Tears streamed down his face but he didn't stop his forward movement.

The master boxed himself into a corner. His gaze shifted back and forth looking for an escape.

Cavan planned to take advantage of it. Pulling the handle up, he tucked it under his arm. Switching the rod to his left hand, he grasped the whip in his right.

He'd seen whips used enough times to have some idea of how to use one. Now, he'd see if he could.

"It's all your fault, isn't it?" Cavan flicked the whip but it went wide and missed his mark.

Just the threat sent the man into a quivering crouch.

"You're responsible for me being kidnapped when I was a kid." He tried again. This time the tip landed on the man's leg.

The howl of pain sent a satisfied shiver through Cavan's body. "You're the one who arranged for me to live with Wainwright. For Mateo, for Samuel and all the others." Another strike found a solid mark on the weasel's face.

The man screamed. His hands covered his face. He hunched over on the floor, his back to Cavan.

"If it weren't for you, I would have had a normal life. And Biton would never have been involved." Tears choked his words. "And he wouldn't have died." Anger lashed out with the whip this time. Boiling rage found its target again and again.

Screams of anguish merged with howls of loss. Over and over, Cavan struck, sometimes finding his mark, sometimes not. It didn't matter any more.

Then hands grabbed him and pulled him away. "Let me go! He deserves to die! Get the fuck off me!"

Blue uniforms, badges, guns... And then strong arms and a familiar body held him tight.

"Cavan, it's okay," Antonio's voice crooned in his ear. "I've got you. You're safe."

Hands rubbed the back of his neck. Sobs robbed his voice, his breath.

"Calm down, Cavan." Antonio rocked him back and forth. "Get a paramedic in here. He's needs a tranquilizer."

"Biton..." Cavan gasped. "He. Killed. Biton."

"Oh God, no, Cavan. Biton's alive."

Cavan's thought he'd heard the words but pent up frustration and anguish from years of pain wouldn't let him focus. "Alive?"

"Yes, alive."

"But he... shot."

"Yes, he was injured but he's alive. And waiting outside." Antonio's arms squeezed him tight. "He wouldn't stay at the hospital. Good thing too, because he helped find you."

"Need to see him." Calm descended like a sledgehammer. His knees gave out. If not for Antonio's grip, he'd have hit the floor.

The rattle of wheels came through the door. Two

men in uniforms took him from Antonio's embrace and lowered him to a bed on wheels.

Paramedics… His mind replayed Antonio's words. A needle pierced his skin. Hands wrapped soft material around his bloody hands. Something stinging touched his battered lip. Floating, he watched the ceiling go by as they wheeled him away.

The heat of the summer day warmed his chilled skin. Biton's face hovered above his.

"Cavan? I'm here, love. Everything will be okay." His hand caressed the side of Cavan's face.

"We need to get him to the hospital, sir."

"Not without me. I'm riding with you."

The paramedic opened his mouth but when Cavan's bandaged fingers wrapped around Biton's hand, he closed it again.

"Don't leave me."

"Never again, love. It's all over."

"Love… I like that," Cavan mumbled.

———

Cavan woke to bright lights and bustling noise. The sharp smell of antiseptic cleaners brought back memories of the night he met Lia, Mr. Casala's slave.

He was alone in the curtained exam room. Where the material parted, he could see someone standing with his back to Cavan. A dark blue oversized t-shirt hung on a frame more familiar than his own. "Biton." The name felt more like a whisper but his master turned and came through the curtain.

"You're awake." A soft kiss brushed his forehead. "How do you feel?"

"Floaty."

Biton laughed. His fingers combed through Cavan's hair. "The paramedics gave you a shot of tranquilizer. You were upset."

Cavan swallowed a lump in his throat. "That man said you were dead."

"I know but I'm not. I'm fine." Biton's hand cupped Cavan's cheek.

Nodding, Cavan relaxed into Biton's touch. "Can we go home?"

"Soon, love. The doctors need to finish examining you. Antonio wants to talk to you as well."

Cavan bit his lip. His memory worked through the medicine and brought back startling images. "Did I… kill that man?" The last three words rushed out.

"No, you didn't. You hurt him pretty bad, but you didn't kill him."

"He's the man I told you about. The man who made Wainwright so mad at Mateo."

"Fairfield is?"

"That's his name?"

"Yes, Simon Fairfield." Biton moved away from Cavan to the curtain. "Antonio, come here a minute."

Mr. Casala slipped through the opening. "Hey, Cavan. How're you feeling?"

"Okay."

"Cavan, tell him about Fairfield."

He took a deep breath then closed his eyes as he

FOREVER

exhaled. "When Mateo first came to Wainwright's house, this man, Fairfield, came to visit. He's the one who hurt Mateo, when he…"

"Raped him?" Antonio supplied the word.

"Yes, raped him. He wasn't happy about Mateo's training and it made Wainwright mad. That's when he beat Mateo to death."

"Thank you, Cavan. That helps a lot." Antonio patted Cavan's leg. "You've done great. I'll have some more questions, so will the district attorney. But for now, you rest and get better."

"Mr. Casala?"

"Yes."

"Will they both get deals now?"

Antonio smiled and shook his head. "They're pointing the finger at each other. They can't talk fast enough. The only deal this time is protection in jail. Most criminals don't like men who abuse children. If they're not isolated from the general population, they'll end up being someone else's slave or dead."

The drugs kept tugging at him, pulling him back into sleep. Forcing his eyes open wide, he nodded. "They need to go away."

"They will. This time, they really will." Antonio nodded then left the exam area.

"I want to go home."

"Soon." A comforting hand caressed Cavan's cheek. "I'll take you home soon." A kiss brushed his forehead.

"Excuse me," a woman's voice interrupted Cavan's drifting peacefulness. "I'm here to see Michael Delany."

Cavan's eyes popped open in time to see Biton's frown before his master turned toward the voice.

"In here, Dr. Merten," another woman's voice answered.

The short round woman came through the parted curtain. "Michael."

"What are you doing here?" Biton's harsh tone made Cavan wince but it bounced off Dr. Merten.

"I'm listed in his medical records as his psychiatrist. The doctor on duty called me." She stalked past Biton to Cavan's bedside. "How are you feeling?"

"Fine." Cavan tried to curl into a ball. Pain from the whip mark on his waist made him hesitate. He didn't want her here.

Biton's gaze darted between Cavan and the doctor. "Dr. Merten, as of now, you are no longer Cavan's therapist." Biton stepped closer to Cavan. His hand blocked hers as she reached for Cavan. "You're fired."

"I'm sorry. You can't fire me. I'm his therapist."

"Well, I pay the bills so that gives me some power over the decision. He doesn't want to see you anymore. You've done nothing but confuse him by insisting he not talk to me about anything."

The woman straightened her back and tilted her head back slightly. "His treatment is confidential. He doesn't have to discuss our conversations."

"Even if he wants to? That's not how I understand psychotherapy. Besides, the things you've been telling him are making him more depressed."

Her gaze darted toward Cavan then back to Biton.

"I've only told him the truth. He can't heal from a life of abuse if someone continues to abuse him." She looked at Cavan again. "You need to learn to live a normal life, Michael. You can't do that with him."

"No," Cavan shook his head. "I'm not leaving. It's my choice. It always has been."

"Your case is delicate and a change of doctors right now could be damaging."

"I don't care what you think, he won't be seeing you again." Biton's glare should have burned Dr. Merten to ashes but she held her ground.

"Dr. Merten…" Cavan whispered. He just wanted to sleep not watch them argue.

"Yes, dear." She leaned over him. A small smile quirked her lips.

"You're fired." With a sigh, Cavan let sleep claim him.

Chapter Eight

Daylight had barely peeked through the windows when Cavan woke. Biton's body snuggled close to his back in the wide soft bed. The last couple of days now seemed like a nightmare, one that was finally over.

Biton's breath snuffled on Cavan's neck. Little movements signaled his awakening—a twitch of his hand on Cavan's stomach, his foot rubbing on Cavan's. His morning erection pressed against Cavan's naked ass.

Heat swirled through Cavan's body and pooled in his groin. His cock responded with enthusiasm.

A deep intake of breath accompanied Biton's arm tightening around Cavan—followed by a gasp of pain.

"Fuck!" Biton rolled onto his back. "Damn shoulder."

Cavan rolled over toward him. "Need some more pain pills?"

Biton squirmed a little then settled. A grimace lined his face. "No, makes me too groggy." He held his arm close to his chest. The white bandage made his naturally tanned skin appear darker. His uninjured arm slid across the small space between him and Cavan. His fingers traced Cavan's swollen lips. "How are you?"

"Happy to be home." Cavan caught Biton's hand in his own. "Glad you're okay." Tears stung his eyes.

"Want to talk about it?"

"When he said you were dead… I…" Even knowing it wasn't true, Cavan's heart skipped a beat and a lump filled his throat.

"It's okay." Biton's hand teased Cavan's shoulder. "You were very brave. Samuel said you rescued him." Biton's fingers threaded between Cavan's. "You could have escaped, gone for help."

Cavan lowered his head. "I thought about it. Fairfield was going to use a whip. All I could think about was getting away."

"But you didn't."

"I waited too long. I heard them coming back and I had to go down into the basement to hide." Cavan shrugged. "I don't know what I would have done if I'd had more time."

"If you hadn't cared, you wouldn't have hesitated. After everything you've been through, that means something. And you defended yourself, you didn't give in to Fairfield. That's a big deal."

"You said it was my choice."

"Come here." Biton's hand tugged at Cavan's.

Snuggling against Biton's uninjured side, Cavan slid his arm across his waist. Biton's arm tightened around him.

"I'm glad you realized that in time."

"Will I still need to see a therapist?" Cavan was relieved Dr. Merten was out of the picture. He didn't want to talk about his life to anyone but Biton.

"Yes, but we'll find someone more sympathetic to your situation and our relationship. I'm sure Dr. Merten was doing what she felt was right but she didn't understand."

"I love you. I want to stay here with you." Cavan needed to hear Biton say he could. His brush with his former life left him feeling stronger but at the same time, more insecure.

Biton kissed his forehead. "I love you, too, and I want you here. No one can make you leave. Do you still want a written contract?"

"No. I don't need it. I think I understand now."

"Understand what?"

"We just made a contract."

"Yes, one that may last forever. Or may not."

"But it's our choice." Cavan pressed his swollen lips against Biton's shoulder. His hand slid down Biton's stomach. The flagging remains of Biton's erection twitched under the sheet.

"What are you doing?" Biton whispered.

"Playing…" Cavan's bandaged hand pressed against Biton's cock through the soft sheet. "Want me to stop?" The warm flesh filled and lengthened.

"No, but we're both a little handicapped. My shoulder, your hands and mouth… We'll need to be creative."

Tiny stitches pulled when Cavan tried to grin. His battered mouth wasn't ready for smiling. "The cuts on my hands aren't bad. They don't hurt much." Cavan pressed harder against the hardening flesh. "You'll tell me if your shoulder hurts too much?" His fingers teased Biton's cock with gentle pulls.

"Uh huh…" Biton sighed. "Just like you'll tell me when we're in the dungeon."

"Because the pain makes the pleasure sweeter."

Biton's arm tightened around him. "That's part of it."

Cavan pressed his erection into Biton's hip. "And giving control to someone else…" He couldn't think of the word he wanted to use. "…frees you."

"Yes, and accepting control freely given is exhilarating."

"So we both feel good…" Cavan wrapped his hand around Biton's hot flesh through the sheet—longer strokes, tighter grip. The pressure caused a sharp stab of pain through his hand but he didn't stop.

Biton's breaths shortened. The muscles in his chest tensed. "Yes…" His breath whispered against Cavan's forehead. "Feels good…"

In spite of his sore mouth, Cavan lifted his face toward Biton. Gentle kisses stung but Cavan didn't care. He was here, safe…home. Something he'd not known how much he missed until he thought he'd lost

259

it again. Gentle turned hungry, needy.

"Easy, Cavan." Biton's fingers tugged Cavan's hair. "Don't make the damage worse. I happen to like the things those lips can do and I want them healed."

"Like yesterday morning?" Cavan rolled his thumb over the tip of Biton's cock. Moisture spotted the sheet.

"Oh, yeah. A great example." His hips pushed his length through Cavan's fist. "But not until your mouth is healed."

The need for pressure against his cock grew. Pressing into Biton's hip wasn't enough. Cavan pulled away from Biton's warmth taking the sheet with him. He straddled his master's hips.

Lining their cocks up together, he leaned forward and pressed his face against Biton's neck.

"Oh, yeah," Biton's moan encouraged Cavan. "That'll work."

Pushing against the tight stomach, he found the pressure he needed. Biton's hand heated Cavan's hip, gripping him tight.

Pleasure curled through his body. Not just the sensual feel of his master's cock against his, not only the need threading through his balls…but the simple feeling of belonging. To this man, in this house, in someone's life.

Need, want, desire and love filled him with a joy greater than his impending orgasm. He was home.

ABOUT THE AUTHOR

By day, Shayla Kersten is a mild-mannered accountant. By night, she's a writer of sexy romances. Torn between genres, Shayla writes erotic stories about hot heroes and their sexy women, as well as hot men and their passionate heroes.

A native of Arkansas, Shayla spent four years in the Army as a missile specialist, stationed in Germany and Oklahoma. After her enlistment was up, she spent eleven years in New York City taking a bite out of the Big Apple. Even her love of theatre and the nightlife of the big city couldn't cure terminal homesickness for the Natural State. In 1995, she returned to her roots in Arkansas.

Shayla now divides her time between her mother, her spoiled rotten critters, her dratted day job and her obsession—writing.

Find Shayla on the web!

Website: www.shaylakersten.com
Facebook: http://www.facebook.com/shaylakersten
Twitter: http://twitter.com/ShaylaKersten

9 781456 592356